CALCULATED RISK

DL WHITE

BOOKS BY DL WHITE

Copyright © 2025 by DL White

Ebook ISBN: 979-8-9907941-9-1

Print ISBN: 979-8-9907941-4-6

Editing by: **A. Kaitesi Tibandebage**

Cover by DL White. Image courtesy Depositphotos

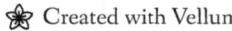 Created with Vellum

AUTHOR'S NOTE

Dear Readers,

Well, here we are once again at publication of another project that excites me, that I am proud to publish and I hope is entertaining. In perilous times, people turn to art. It is my hope that readers new and old will consider Books by DL White as a respite and comfort.

Calculated Risk follows Imani, a financial analyst whose carefully structured life is upended when she begins teaching workshops at a youth center, and Desmond, the center's director who carries the weight of his past while building a future for young adults. Their story unfolds against the backdrop of a vibrant community fighting to keep its sanctuary alive.

While this is primarily a love story, I love a secondary story and an external conflict, so this story also examines how our choices and circumstances beyond our control shape who we become. The novel explores family bonds, community activism, and love after loss.

Much of Desmond's journey and the Beyond Bars support group were inspired by Ian Bick's podcast ***Locked***

In with Ian Bick. Through watching Ian's raw, honest conversations with formerly incarcerated individuals rebuilding their lives on YouTube, I gained invaluable insights that shaped not only Desmond's character but also the authenticity of the re-entry experience and the power of community support.

Please note the following content warnings and please take care when reading if any of these are triggers or deal breakers for you:

- Discussions of illness and death
- Sexual intercourse on the page
- Themes of betrayal
- References to substance use
- Mentions of police encounters and the criminal justice system

This story contains mature themes and is intended for adult readers.

I hope you love spending time with Imani, Desmond, and the colorful cast of characters at Bright Pathways Youth Center.

If you enjoy this work, please tell a friend or six and don't forget to drop a good word at all the important places: your personal social media, Goodreads, The StoryGraph.

Thank you for your time, I hope you enjoy this story!

DL White

CALCULATED RISK

When heartbreak leads to love...

All her life, Imani Thatcher has played it safe, making the smart moves that landed her a prime spot at one of Atlanta's top financial firms. When heartbreak shatters her carefully planned world, she finds herself questioning everything she thought she knew about love and life.

Desmond Taylor has enough on his plate keeping Bright Pathways Youth Center running and Atlanta's at-risk teens off the streets. A polished financial analyst from the high gloss end of Atlanta should be the last thing on his mind, but from the moment she walks through his doors, he cannot deny the electricity between them.

When it comes to matters of the heart, love is always a calculated risk—and the biggest payoffs come when you put everything on the line.

CALCULATED RISK

ONE

IMANI

"I BET the next time I tell you somebody's acting funny, you'll believe me." Casey's sharp whisper sliced through the rumbling notes of the funeral organ. "Won't ya?"

"Will you hush?" Imani leaned in, a polite smile masking her irritation as she glanced at their companions in the church balcony.

Below them, the family of Julian Carver made their solemn procession into the sanctuary, taking their places in the gleaming front pew. Imani's gaze locked on an elegant figure sweeping in last, dressed in black from head to toe—a veiled wide-brimmed hat, a chic yet somber dress, towering red-soled heels. She paused at the casket, whispering to a man who, mere days ago, pulsed with life and love and promises.

Then she snapped open a large, black fan and turned to her seat, ushers braced to catch her should she crumple in sorrow.

"That must be the wife, huh?" Casey whispered.

"Vivian," Imani confirmed.

"Mmmhmmm. He got kids too?"

"They're down there." Imani indicated the row of adults flanking Vivian.

"Hell, them ain't no kids. Those are grown ass people." Casey sighed, flipping through the funeral program and flapping the stereotypical Martin Luther King, Jr. paper fan on a wooden stick.

As the pastor began his sermon, Imani tried to focus on his words, but her thoughts kept drifting. She glanced over the balcony edge, observing the family's interactions—silent nods, hands held tight, maintaining composure under the weight of public grief. His voice rose with fervor as he spoke.

"Julian Carver was a man who assumed many roles and wore many hats," he boomed, his orator's rhythm and cadence kicking in, echoing up through the high ceilings of the church.

Two weeks prior, Imani had been on the phone with Julian.

They had met at a mutual friend's wedding in Atlanta and hit it off immediately. Though they lived states away, their connection felt effortless. Despite his job running a successful manufacturing plant in Raleigh and her demanding job as a financial analyst in Atlanta, they found ways to make it work. Frequent video calls, surprise visits when time allowed it. Imani truly believed that they were building something special together.

After a few months of dating, the relationship had advanced quickly. Julian began talking about their future, and he'd been not-so-gently encouraging her to pull up stakes and move to North Carolina to be with him.

"You know how I feel about you, Imani," he'd said. "I can't imagine being without you. I'm ready for that next step. Commitment. Being together full-time."

Imani swooned at his words. They had only been dating for a short time, but it felt like much longer to her heart. Julian was everything she never knew she wanted—kind, funny, genuinely interested in getting to know her, and though he was nearly twenty years her senior, had no problems satisfying her every sexual need.

The idea of uprooting her life and moving to a new state for someone she barely knew was daunting. Leaving behind the life she had built for herself seemed reckless. Imani was hesitant, her mind going back and forth between excitement and caution, giddy new love and common sense.

"I'm not sure I'm ready for that yet," she'd finally admitted. "I mean... I don't think we are ready for that."

Julian paused for a moment before responding. "You're right. We haven't been together long, but I've been alive and around these relationship streets long enough to know that I don't want to miss out on something good. I promise you, I have never felt this way about anyone before. And I know you feel it too."

He wasn't wrong. She had felt it. She didn't completely trust it, though. And there were practical concerns to consider, like her job that paid well and gave her stability.

"Maybe I can talk to my boss about teleworking," she'd mused. "I could keep my place and stay here when I have to be in Atlanta."

"See, that sharp mind is working," he'd replied confidently. "And if they won't let you work remote, you know I've got you, baby."

Imani's eyes rolled. He was laying it on thick. The idea was tempting, though. "I'll think about it," she promised.

"Well, think fast. I can't wait to wake up next to you every morning."

Imani chuckled, remembering their last morning together a few weeks prior. They'd almost worked the headboard off of her bed. She could still feel his fingertips on her skin, the softness of his lips as he teased and titillated until she was breathless and begging for more.

"I bet you can't," she replied with a sly smile. "I know how you like to wake up."

Julian let out a low growl, the sound rumbling across the line. "Don't tease me, woman. Not when I can't reach out and touch you."

They had laughed and talked until late into the night, making plans and dreaming big.

Days later, he hadn't made his usual check-ins. Their routine was to reach out several times a day, sometimes just to say hello, I love you, I'll call you tonight. At the very least, it was their way of staying connected despite the distance between them.

She called and got no answer. She left voicemails and sent texts with no response. No email, no gifts, none of the usual hallmarks of what she had known in a long-distance relationship with Julian Carver. He was a very busy man, but he was not one to go more than a day without communicating.

Imani tried not to panic, but it was hard not knowing what was going on with the man she loved, a man she was about to upend her life to be with.

After days of silence, she had reached her breaking point. She called his work line at Carver Manufacturing and asked for him directly—a thing she was never to do, but she was worried and desperate. Something was wrong.

"Oh...you haven't heard," said the Southern-tinged, melancholy voice on the other end of the line.

"I guess I haven't," Imani said, afraid to ask for clarification. "What haven't I heard?"

The voice on the other exhaled a deep, shuddering breath. "Julian—Mr. Carver—he's gone."

"Gone. As in..."

"He...died. Suddenly and unexpectedly."

Imani's heart stopped beating. Her world had crumbled in an instant. "When?"

"Just a few days ago. I can get you in touch with his wife. She's asked that we funnel any calls or condolences through her."

Wife.

She had never even suspected that he could be married. There was no hint of a ring on his finger, no mention of a wife on his social media, and most of all, he had never once referenced even being in a relationship with another woman, let alone married.

Julian, the man she'd been dating for a large part of the year, who had frequently come to Atlanta, who had flown her to Raleigh and hosted her in his condo, who had wined and dined and gifted and sweet-talked her and ravished her body...had been married.

The. Whole. Damn. Time.

"Are you there, ma'am?" the person on the other end of the line asked, breaking through her stunned silence.

"Yes," she heard herself reply. Her voice sounded distant, even to her own ears. "I'm sorry, you mentioned his wife..."

"Yes. Vivian must be so distraught, and someone else should really handle these details, but she's not the kind of person to relinquish control. Shall I connect you?"

"I... I, uhm..." Imani stuttered through a reply, then laid a hand over her galloping heart to get her bearings. "I just wondered if you knew when the service would be?"

With shaking fingers, she wrote down the name of the funeral home, which would list the church where Julian's service would be held.

The very next phone call Imani made was to her best friend, Casey Joyner.

"I told you something was up with him."

Casey, a middle-aged Black woman with a buxom chest and ass to spare, had thrown on her stylish cat-eye glasses and a curly wig and come right over in her cotton two-piece pajama set, carting pints of Häagen-Dazs ice cream and Stella Rosa wine in a big black handbag.

"You told me to mind my business, but I should have ignored you, mmmhmm." She hummed, swiping a tube of Fenty beauty gloss over her thick lips. "I should have run a background check the minute he started talking about you moving up there."

"Yes. Well." Imani popped the cork on the wine and took a swig right from the bottle, ignoring the cup Casey offered her. "You were right. How long are you going to crow about it?"

"Until I also am dead."

Imani sagged, too wrung out to volley back. She felt numb and sick at the same time. The man she had fallen for, who had swept her off her feet and treated her like a princess, had been living a double life with a wife and family.

"I can't even believe this shit. Men are still doing this? Still lying, still pretending, still having their cake and eating it too?" Imani shook her head, her cheeks shiny with tears. "I thought he loved me."

"Him loving you ain't had nothing to do with being faithful to his wife." Casey moved from the couch to the loveseat where Imani was curled up with her wine glass and pulled her close, hugging her tight. "You know what I always say, 'Mani. Some men are just cold ass mutha-fuckahs."

They sat on the couch together, eating ice cream and drinking wine as Imani poured out all of her feelings about Julian.

"So when's the service?" Casey asked.

Imani reached for the slip of paper she'd used to scribble down the information and handed it to her. "I'm going," she said quietly.

Casey reared back. "For what? You do not need to be in that room, baby girl. With his wife, his family, all his loved ones blubbering and carrying on? Are you trying to be in a Tyler Perry film?"

"Maybe I need to see it for myself. See him one last time. And maybe...I need to see *her*."

Casey arched a brow, setting down her wine glass. "And do what? Compare yourself to her? Confront her? Throw a fit in the middle of a funeral? That's messy, Imani. You're better than that."

"Am I, though?" Imani asked, then grabbed the bottle of Stella and topped off their glasses before toasting Julian one last time.

The six-hour drive from Atlanta to Raleigh, North Carolina was long, but Imani felt she had to be there. For closure. To say goodbye to the man she thought she knew, thought she was in love with.

And to sneak a peek at Mrs. Carver.

She was, in fact, nothing like Imani expected her to be. She could maybe figure Julian stepping out on an older, haggard woman, but Mrs. Carver was none of that. She was elegant, her makeup flawless, not a hair out of place. Vivian's stoicism was almost unnerving.

The service was a blur of hymns and eulogies that painted Julian in hues too vibrant to recognize. The man they spoke of was a devoted husband, a loving father, a pillar of his community. Imani listened, her heart sinking with each speaker that shared a story about a Julian Carver that bore no semblance to the man she'd known—a man now revealed to be an artifice, a man fabricated to attract her.

As Vivian and her children wept for their loss, Imani felt like an intruder. She had come seeking closure but instead found herself feeling guilt and shame for the role she unknowingly played in Julian's deception.

After nearly an hour of listening to the preacher droning his sermon, Imani felt Casey's hand squeeze hers. "You're not planning on throwing yourself on the body, are you?" she whispered.

Imani's eyes rolled in irritation. "Of course not."

"Then let's get out of here. We have a long drive back."

She agreed. They should leave before anyone noticed she had come. They rose and tiptoed out of the balcony, down the stairs, and into the vestibule, where they finally felt like they could breathe.

"Whew. This Yitty is cutting into my kitty and I can't breathe. I want to change back into my riding clothes." Casey looked left and right, already pulling at the zipper of her dress.

"Let's just stop at a restroom on the way out of town," said Imani. "I want to get out of here."

"I'm not changing in an Exxon bathroom—"

A glacial voice stopped them cold. "Excuse me."

Imani and Casey whipped around, eyes wide and mouths open, to find Vivian Carver standing there, gloved hands clasped tightly.

"Mrs. Carver," said Imani, moving toward. "I'm so sorry for your—"

"Shut up," she snapped. Imani froze mid-step. Vivian's eyes were cold and unyielding. "I know exactly who you are. I've been through his phone, his texts, his email, his credit cards. I've seen his cute little bachelor pad downtown. I know Julian fed you a deluded fantasy that you might be his wife someday. Well, surprise, little girl."

Vivian's eyes traveled the length of her belted tea-length dress. Imani could tell she was trying hard to find fault with it but couldn't, so she sneered out of spite and anger. Her words dripped with venom, each syllable a dagger aimed directly at her heart.

"You will not stand over my husband's corpse, play-acting the grieving widow. You have no place here," she hissed, her eyes blazing. "I want you gone this instant before I file a claim for every tacky piece of jewelry he ever bought you and sue you for every penny of our fortune—money he and I earned *together*—that he spent trying to convince you that you ever had a chance to become Mrs. Julian Carver."

"I didn't know," Imani rasped, fighting to steady her voice. Tears brimmed in her eyes as she met Vivian's steely gaze. "I didn't know he was married, I promise. I only came to pay my respects. I thought..."

The foolish, pitiful extent of what she'd thought crashed over her. What had she thought? That Julian would never lie to her? That she'd finally found a wonderful man to settle down with? That they had a future?

"Whatever you thought?" Vivian's lips thinned into a merciless line. "You thought wrong. Julian may have hidden his real life well, but you are not welcome here. Please leave, and if you know what's good for you, you'll forget Julian Carver ever existed."

"Yeah, we were leaving anyway," Casey interjected, propelling Imani out the doors to their waiting car.

"What the hell crawled up her ass?" Imani fumed as the stately Cadillac purred to life. Casey's husband had insisted on sending them to Raleigh in style.

"Probably the knowledge that the man she's spittin' mad about was keeping company with a hot young Atlanta thing."

Imani recoiled at the label—the other woman. The homewrecker. She had always prided herself on being strong and independent, but now she felt like nothing more than a pawn in someone else's game. She had been so naive, so foolish.

Miles slipped by, the city giving way to green framed by the occasional billboard advertising barbecue joints and local attractions. Imani stared out the window, her reflection a ghostly overlay on the passing scenery. She felt hollow, each mile taking her further not just from Julian's funeral but from the dreams she admitted she had begun to indulge in.

"I hear that mind ticking over there. Rollin' things around. You need to get your head on straight. Figure out your plan for moving on."

"You're right." Imani inhaled, steeling her spine. "I need to figure out what's next. And I have to stop letting this situation live rent-free in my head. It's done. Over. Moving on."

Casey nodded approvingly, her fingers tight around the wide steering wheel. "That's the spirit, baby girl. You need a fresh start. Something to throw yourself into."

TWO

DESMOND

AFTERNOONS AT BRIGHT Pathways Youth Center were never calm.

The renovated community center, once a crumbling husk, now pulsed with the rowdy energy of teens that made the safe haven a home away from home. The single-story structure was a sanctuary for those who were often overlooked by the world.

As the clock struck four-thirty, the front door burst open, ushering in a pack of young men fresh from the basketball courts. In the lounge reserved for the older center attendees, laughter and chatter swelled to a cacophony, punctuated by the clack of pool balls and the droning TV.

A few lone souls sat at the tables, hunched over books or laptops, trying to drown out the noise.

"Alright, alright, listen up!" Desmond's baritone sliced through the din. He grabbed the remote, silencing the TV. "Have a seat. Let's get started."

Dragging a chair to the mismatched couches, he watched the crew settle in, jostling for space, balancing heaping plates and sloshing cups overflowing with fizzy soda.

"How did everybody's day go?" asked Desmond. His warm, brown eyes bounced around the circle as he waited for responses. After a few moments of pronounced chewing, a stocky young man raised a hand.

"You ain't gotta raise your hand, Caleb," joked another group member. "Just go, man."

"Caesar is right. You don't have to raise your hand," Desmond corrected, then nodded at Caleb. "Talk to me."

"A'ight, so boom. In Econ, our teacher is always talking about life stuff. Like how much eggs cost and the minimum wage. I was just thinking that like... I don't know what the fu—heck he's talking about, man."

"First of all, you don't have to censor yourself in here. This place is for you, about you. You heard me?"

"A'ight, then. I don't know what the fuck Mr. Lawson be talking about."

"And that's concerning to you? To all of you?" Desmond scanned the room again, observing the nods. "So why you think, out of all the kids rolling through here, I picked this crew to meet with?"

"We're your favorites?" someone tossed out.

"Cute, but nah. Try again."

A few shrugs, then a mumbled, "I don't know," filled the silence.

"Caleb, how old are you?"

"Seventeen. I'll be eighteen in the spring."

"Caesar?"

"Seventeen."

"Deja?"

"I just turned seventeen," she replied.

Desmond fixed his gaze on the newest addition to their group. "What's your name?" he asked.

"Chloe," she replied.

"And how old are you?" Desmond probed further.

"Seventeen," Chloe responded.

Desmond shifted to lean his elbows on his knees, hands clasped. "What else do you have in common? And at eighteen, what happens to each of you?"

"We're all in foster care," Caleb replied. "And we get kicked off the government's tit."

The room erupted into laughter.

"That's pretty much it," said Desmond. "Even if you have great foster parents, once you reach a certain age, they stop receiving financial support from the government to care for you. They might not even have enough space in their home, especially if they want to take in another child."

Desmond paused and stood, sliding his hands into the pockets of loose-cut jeans. "It's important that you know how to manage your life if you end up in a situation where you have to support yourself. You need to know these life skills that your teacher refers to. So..."

He walked to the desk shoved into the corner of the room and picked up a yellow legal pad and a pen. "This group is about crowdsourcing the concerns you might have about life after foster care. You tell me what you need, and I'll link with the community to hook you up. Applying for jobs, basic cooking tips, looking for an apartment, how to pick a good roommate...whatever you feel like you need to know before you're out of the system, we'll use this group to find the answers."

He leaned against the desk and scanned the room again.

"So lay it on me. What do you want to know? What do you need to know before you're out there on your own?"

The group was silent for a moment, the weight of their upcoming independence hanging heavily in the air. Then Deja spoke up, her voice quieter than usual. "What if we don't even know what we need to know?"

Desmond barked a laugh. "I'd say you sound like most of us adults. On top of that, realizing that you don't know shit about shit is stressful. Ain't it, Caleb?"

"You ain't even lyin'," said Caleb, his brows riding high on his forehead.

"Okay, so what's the first thing we're adding to this list?"

"Well..." Chloe piped up. "I have a little weekend job and a savings account, but I want to know more about how to manage money. I want to get my own apartment, and I want to know what I might have to pay for, 'cause I know it's a hell of a lot more to pay than rent."

"Alright, so we need to find someone who can teach you about checking and savings accounts, and how to budget expenses as an independent young adult."

"Why can't you just teach us, Des?" Caesar asked. "We're already here in this group. You run this place and you're old. You must know stuff."

Desmond was quiet for a long moment as he gazed at the group of teens on the cusp of adulthood in front of him.

"For reasons that I'm not going to get into," he finally quietly replied, "I can't. But I'll find a person to help you."

The group exchanged unsure glances before Desmond continued. "In the meantime, let's keep adding to our list of skills and knowledge that you'll need to be a successful member of society."

Deja, who had been quiet, spoke up again. "I want to know about school, like college stuff. Not just getting in, but how to pay for it. Scholarships, work-study, financial aid, grants."

"Got it. Education opportunities and financial support for college," Desmond scribbled across the notepad. "We can definitely get into that. What else?"

Together, the group developed a healthy list of skills and seminars to attend over the next few months. As the group dispersed, Desmond released a sigh that had long been pent up inside him. When the room was empty, he pulled his phone from a pocket, scrolled to a number, and tapped it.

"Taylor." A crisp voice backed by road noise filled the room via the phone's speaker. "I told you, you don't have to check in anymore. Your release is no longer supervised."

Desmond grinned. "Ain't nobody checking in with you, Gary. What you up to?"

"The usual. Regulatin'."

Desmond laughed. "So, running down wayward parolees?"

"You know it. What's up? I haven't heard from you in a minute."

"Well..." Desmond pushed out a sigh, leaning back in his chair. "I've got this group here at the youth center. All kids about to turn eighteen and graduate high school—"

"And get kicked off the system."

"Not all of them. Sometimes kids can get placed until they're twenty-one, but yeah, for most kids, eighteen is the line, especially if they're not close with their foster parents. Today, they started asking about life skills stuff. Bank accounts, credit cards, all that."

"They're asking *you* about life skills?"

"That's why I'm calling. I do alright for some topics, but

they want advice on money management and...I feel uncomfortable advising anyone on the subject of money."

"Why? You did your time and your record is clear. Nothing in your case file says you can't tell kids how to open a checking account."

Desmond rubbed his forehead, feeling a familiar tension headache building. "I don't even want to touch this. I don't want any appearance of wrongdoing here. I was calling to see if you had a connect, someone who might come in for a few weeks and talk to the kids about personal finance."

"I might know a few people," said Gary. "I've got a friend that runs a finance firm; I'll make a phone call. Any money in it? If so, I'll come teach it."

"Nah," Desmond answered. "This is strictly a volunteer position. Pizza for the group is a stretch these days."

"Fine, cheap ass. Let me work on it. I'll get back to you. You talked to your brother lately?"

"No," said Desmond with a heavy sigh. "And I don't plan to. I gotta run, G. Hit me back with some options."

He hung up, cutting off Gary's reply. The phone landed on the blotter with a thud. His gaze drifted back to the window, his own tired face reflected against the evening sky outside.

Desmond stood, shuffling papers around on his desk, stacking them together in an attempt to regain his focus. The weight of his past was an albatross around his neck, but Desmond knew he was where he needed to be. He couldn't change what had already happened, but he could help shape the future for those coming up behind him.

As he passed the window, he looked out at the south-west Atlanta neighborhood, its familiarity an unusual comfort. The streetlights flickered on, casting golden pools on the sidewalk. His mind wandered back to the kids in the group. Each of them was at a turning point, so full of potential yet so burdened by the invisible strings of their circumstances. Desmond felt a deep responsibility toward them, a desire to guide them through these critical moments.

He turned away from the window and glanced at the community notice board plastered with flyers—job training programs, GED prep classes, free health clinic days. Pausing, he took down an old flyer and replaced it with a fresh sheet announcing the upcoming personal finance workshop, hoping Gary would come through with a volunteer.

Turning off the lights and locking the double doors of the community center, Desmond felt the evening chill seep through his jacket. The streets were empty, save for the occasional car that whizzed by.

Pulling his collar up, he started the walk home.

THREE

IMANI

THE STACCATO RHYTHM of stilettos echoed through the parking garage at Richardson & Burke Finance, each step a ticking reminder of the turmoil churning.

Imani stepped into her office, dropping her designer tote on her desk. The space was small but efficient, with windows offering a sparkling view of Atlanta's morning skyline. Her mahogany desk gleamed, meticulously organized, not a single paper out of place.

Before settling into a leather ergonomic desk chair, she paused to view her framed degrees hung in a precise grid: an Associate's in Accounting, Bachelor of Science in Finance, countless certifications. Hard-earned trophies of academic excellence.

Or a wall of sheer mockery because she had yet to figure out how a person so learned, so intelligent could fall for Julian Carver's lies.

She had moved past sadness days ago. Now she was

furious, and it was beginning to affect her job—just about the only stable thing in her life.

The cursor on the screen blinked incessantly, waiting for input. Imani stared at it, willing the words of the memo she was supposed to be writing to materialize. But her mind wandered, as it often did these days, to Julian. His laugh, his smile, the way he'd—

"Nope," she muttered, shaking her head. *Get your mind right, girl.*

She'd barely typed a paragraph when a knock on her door jolted her back to reality.

"Hey, Imani." It was Tanya, one of the assistants. "Conrad wants to see you in his office."

Imani's stomach dropped. She'd been dreading this. Her billable hours were down, and her work hadn't been up to her usual standard in weeks. It was only a matter of time before someone noticed.

"Thank you, Tanya. I'll be right there."

Smoothing her pencil skirt and pulling her blazer closed to fasten the button, Imani picked up her laptop, a notebook, and a pen, then headed down the hall to her boss's office.

The walk to Conrad Richardson's office felt like a march to the gallows. She conjured up worst-case scenarios despite knowing she was a rock star in the company with only a few weeks of less-than-stellar work. The odds that she was being fired were low. But not zero.

"Come in," Conrad called as she knocked.

He was seated behind a massive desk in business casual wear—which at the firm meant a short-sleeved golf shirt bearing the company logo and khaki pants with vegan leather sneakers. His wire-rimmed glasses perched on the end of his nose as he peered into an oversized monitor.

Imani took a seat, her back ramrod straight, hands clasped tightly in her lap.

"Conrad, I—"

He held up a hand, silencing her. "I've called you in because—"

"I know my work hasn't been the best lately," she blurted out, unable to contain herself. "My billable hours are down and I'm behind on submitting invoices, but I recently lost a good friend and I just haven't been on my A-game. But I promise, I'm getting it together. I—"

"Imani," Conrad interrupted. He removed his glasses and focused steely grey eyes on her. "This isn't a disciplinary meeting. Well, not the kind you seem to be expecting."

She blinked, caught off guard. "It's...not?"

"No," he said, leaning back in his chair. "Though now that you mention it, you have been distracted and quiet lately. You say you lost a good friend recently? Are you alright?"

Imani swallowed hard. "Yes, sir. Everything's fine. He just...meant a lot to me and I'm adjusting."

Conrad nodded. "Loss is never easy to navigate, especially when you're trying to maintain a demanding career. Please accept my condolences. I wish you'd told me. You could have taken a few days of bereavement."

Imani felt a lump forming in her throat but forced it down. *Bereavement to mourn her married lover?* "Thank you," she choked out.

"Anyway, the reason I called you in," Conrad continued, mercifully changing the subject, "is that we're nearing the end of the year, and I'm reviewing the pro bono hours that each associate is required to complete. Now is the time to jump into a project if you need to satisfy your hours—and you do. You haven't logged any hours this year."

Imani's eyes widened. It had been a very busy year of back-to-back projects, plus Julian had occupied so much of her time. The year had flown by quickly and, to be fair, she'd completely forgotten about the firm's pro bono requirement.

"I... I'm so sorry, Conrad. It completely slipped my mind. I'll find some organizations to donate time to—"

He lifted a finger to quiet her while a smile played at the corners of his mouth. "As it happens, I have the perfect opportunity for you."

Imani's shoulders sagged. She was hoping to rope Casey into hooking her up with an easy project she could coast through.

"A friend called me last week looking for some help from a finance professional," Conrad said, pulling his glasses from his face. From a pocket, he retrieved a handkerchief and mindlessly rubbed the lenses as he spoke. "He knows of a community center in southwest Atlanta that serves at-risk youth. You know, kids in various economically disadvantaged situations that might not graduate high school. They need someone to conduct workshops for the group. We hammered out a six-week commitment, one evening a week."

Imani's enthusiasm waned even more. Southwest Atlanta was across town and a world away from her Midtown condo. And financial literacy for at-risk youth? Surely Conrad thought more of her time and expertise than teaching teenagers how to balance a checkbook.

"I...see," she said, trying to keep the disappointment out of her voice. "And...you think I'd be a good fit for this?"

"I think it would be an excellent opportunity for you, Imani. It'll fulfill your pro bono requirement, of course. But more than that, I think it might be good for you to offer some expertise to the younger generation. And maybe spending some time developing a protégé will perk you up a bit."

Imani was set to argue. She didn't really have the time to dedicate to teenagers who wanted pointers on how to spend and save money. And she didn't need to be *perked up*, thank you very much. But Conrad's expression told her this wasn't a request.

"Of course," she said, plastering a smile on her lips. "I'd be happy to help."

"Excellent." Conrad beamed, sliding his glasses back up his nose. "I'll have Tanya forward the details. Your first session is this evening."

"This *evening*?" Imani echoed, her voice rising.

"Will that be a problem?"

"No, no problem at all," she lied smoothly. "I'll be there."

By the time Imani climbed into her BMW, she was exhausted. She'd spent the afternoon catching up on the work she'd been slacking on for the past few weeks while mourning a man that had been lying to her. The email from Tanya had come so late in the afternoon that she didn't have time to go home and change. She had no choice but to head straight to her first session at Bright Pathways.

The GPS chirped, guiding her out of Atlanta's business district and into the grittier landscape south of the inter-state. As the neighborhoods changed around her, Imani felt a twinge of...

What was that?

Guilt? Discomfort?

She'd grown up comfortably middle class in the suburbs. As the daughter of two professionals, attending college was not an option. Her path had been paved and her college fund had been set at birth. While she'd worked hard for everything she had, she also knew she'd been born with advantages many others didn't have.

The Bright Pathways Youth Center was a squat, single-story building that had seen better days. Fresh paint and new signage couldn't quite hide the years of wear and tear. Imani parked her car, double-checking that she'd locked it, and approached the entrance.

Fluorescent lights buzzed overhead, casting a harsh glow on the worn linoleum floor. A receptionist glanced up from her phone. "Can I help you?"

"I'm looking for..." Imani consulted her phone, scrolling for Tanya's email. "Desmond Taylor?"

"Oh, right. They said somebody was coming by. Sign in." She nodded her head toward a sheet of lined notebook paper and a pen with no cap laying on the counter. "Then go on through those double doors to the lounge at the end of the hall."

Imani followed the shrieks of laughter and high-pitched chatter. At the end of the hall, she found a large room filled with foosball and ping-pong tables on one side and a group of mismatched couches and chairs on the other. A large steel desk wedged into a corner was a serving area for the boxes of pizza and garlic knots.

She hesitated in the doorway, feeling out of place. The man in the center of the room caught sight of her. He didn't smile, but his countenance wasn't unfriendly. He tipped his head up and waved her into the room as he made his way over to her, weaving through the teenagers scattered about.

"You must be Imani," he said, extending a hand, his voice carrying easily over the chatter. His grip was firm, his palm calloused. He was tall with warm brown skin, closely cropped hair and beard, and a muscular build. He radiated an easy confidence that immediately drew Imani's eye. "Desmond Taylor."

"Nice to meet you," Imani replied, forcing a smile.

"I know this came at you last-minute," Desmond said. "You don't have to pretend this is where you want to spend a Thursday night."

His words caught Imani off guard. She blinked, unsure how to respond. "I... I'm sorry?" she stammered.

His lips tipped into the first hint of a smile. "I know how these things work. Some higher-up at your firm gets guilted into helping out a downtrodden agency and he eenie-meenie-miney-mo ropes a lowly associate into doing pro bono work on his behalf. You don't have to pretend to be thrilled about it."

"I'm not a lowly associate," Imani replied, her tone sharper than she'd intended it to be. "I'm a senior financial analyst. I was told you have individuals on the cusp of adulthood who need guidance. I'm genuinely happy to help. If we could get started, that would be great."

Desmond's brows rose. "Alright, then. That's what I'm talking about." He turned to face the room, shouting over everyone. "Hey, everybody! Listen up!"

The noise slowly died down as all eyes turned to Desmond and Imani.

"We have a guest," Desmond continued. "This is Ms. Imani. She's a senior financial analyst who will be with us for the next six weeks to answer your questions about money."

All eyes turned to Imani, and she suddenly felt over-dressed and out of place in her designer suit and heels.

"First of all, please call me Imani," she began. "I'm sure I will learn your names along the way. I am a senior analyst at a finance firm, which is a fancy way to say I guide businesses in decisions about how to spend money to earn profit. That makes me qualified to answer your questions about how to enter the world as a money-savvy individual."

A chorus of greetings ranging from enthusiastic to indifferent met this announcement.

"How much money you make?"

The question, blunt and unexpected, came from a girl with bright purple braids.

"Deja," Desmond chided gently, trying not to laugh. "Let's keep our questions appropriate and relevant."

Deja shrugged, unrepentant. "You said to ask what we wanted to know. I want to know how much she makes to be pushing that BMW and wearing Hanifa and Manolos to work."

Imani couldn't help her laughter. "It's okay," she said to Desmond. "It's a fair question if I'm here to answer questions about money."

She settled onto the couch next to Deja, who turned toward her with rapt attention.

"The answer is...it depends. People with my job can make anywhere from $80,000 a year to several million, depending on where they work, what kind of clients they work with, and the difficulty of the work they do. I earn a salary, which is a set amount of money. I also earn a bonus based on performance on projects I complete during the year and how much I help the company bring in. I use bonuses to buy things I like... mostly designer dresses and shoes. And bags. I love a nice bag."

"I want a Brandon Blackwood so bad," said a girl at the back of the room.

"Okay, so...answer the question. Where do you fall on that scale?" This was from a lanky young man with a mischievous grin up front.

"Caesar," Desmond warned, but Imani held up a hand.

"I appreciate the curiosity," she said. "Low six figures. I won't be more specific than that, but I earn enough to live comfortably, to have money in savings, a healthy amount in my 401(k), and diverse investments. I can afford nice things, but I'll tell you a secret: I buy items at closeouts and discounts. Neiman Marcus has sales and takes Affirm. You know what I'm saying?"

"A sale hate to see you coming," Deja said, nodding. "You're good with your money. You can make what you have stretch."

"Precisely. And I'm good with my clients' money, which means I can tell you how to be good with yours." This elicited a few laughs from the group, and Imani felt her shoulders drop. "So, what questions can I answer for this group?" she asked, bracing herself for more personal financial inquiries.

A quiet girl in the back raised her hand. "What made you want to be...whatever you are? That sounds boring to me."

Imani paused, considering. It had been a long time since she'd really thought about that. "Well...what sounds fun and interesting to you? What fills you with excitement and passion and makes you think you could do it for the rest of your life?"

She shrugged. "I like stuff about the body. Thought about being a doctor. Something in medicine, but...I don't know."

"That's fair. At seventeen, I didn't know either. But I did know I was good with numbers and that I wanted a career that would give me stability and independence. When I got to college, I started exploring fields that would give me that. I ended up here."

The questions continued, ranging from the serious—*"How do I start building credit?"*—to the ridiculous—*"Can you make me a million dollars?"* More than an hour passed quickly, and Desmond called an end to the session.

"Alright, everybody. Get out of here so I can go home. Next week, we'll dig a little deeper."

Imani added, "Maybe we could start with basic book-keeping, since that's a skill that can benefit you now. You're all of age to work, and some of you may need guidance on what to do with that fat paycheck you're about to get."

"We know you're joking about that," said Caleb. "The government takes like half of your paycheck."

"See? I can skip over the first part of my lesson already—earnings and deductions."

As the teens filed out, calling goodbyes and thank yous, Imani grabbed her bag by the handles and turned to find herself face to face with Desmond.

"I think you survived," he said, his eyes twinkling.

"I think I did better than survive."

"True. Not many people can hold their attention for that long, let alone get them asking questions."

"They're very...inquisitive."

Desmond laughed, a rich, deep sound that Imani found herself wanting to hear again. "I usually go with nosy, but I'll let you think they're nice for a week. I'm about to close up, so I'll walk you out."

They fell into step together heading toward the exit. Desmond closed doors along the way, snapping off lights as they walked.

"I appreciate you coming in for a few weeks to help out," he said, pulling the double doors closed and keying the door lock and the deadbolt. "They'll give a little color to your life, if nothing else."

Imani caught the slight and smiled. "My life isn't as beige as you might think," she defended. "Even though you did peg me right—pro bono work is a requirement at my company—this was refreshing."

The evening air was warm, tinged with the scent of nearby trees. Desmond matched her slow pace, his hands shoved in the pockets of his jeans. His long-sleeved shirt was loose but not so loose that she didn't notice the bulge of muscles through the fabric. As they reached the parking lot, Imani was surprised to find she was reluctant to leave.

Instead, she asked, "So, you run this center?"

"Yeah." Desmond stopped beside her car. "The director job has gone through a few hands in recent years. It doesn't make money, and we don't get a lot of support. I guess it doesn't do much for anyone but the kids that come here. It's been my life for the last few years, though. It means a lot to me."

"It shows," Imani replied. "The kids really respond to you. I can already tell that you do an amazing job here."

"Thanks," he replied, his voice gruff with emotion. "A labor of love, they call it?"

They stood in silence for a moment, the night air filled with the distant sounds of traffic and the occasional bark of a dog.

"So. I should let you go. Assuming they didn't scare you away...same time next week?" Desmond asked.

"I'll be here," Imani promised. She looked around, noticing the lot was empty. "Are you waiting for a ride? Can I give you a lift somewhere?"

"Nah, thanks. I live a few blocks from here, so I usually walk."

He lived close to the center? In...this neighborhood?

Imani felt her cheeks warm, realizing how judgmental her thoughts had been. "Well. Have a good night then."

Desmond nodded, a knowing look in his eyes. "You too, Imani. Drive safe."

As she pulled out of the parking lot, Imani was embarrassed. Desmond had seen right through her. Her presumptions about the neighborhood, about him, about the kids all rang shallow.

The drive home was quiet, her usual playlist forgotten. For the first time in weeks, she wasn't turning the situation with Julian over in her mind. Instead, her thoughts skipped right over him to the lively group at Bright Pathways, to Deja's blunt questions and Caleb's cheeky grin and to the shy, quiet girl in the back.

And to Desmond. His brown eyes seemed to skewer her as if he saw through a carefully constructed facade. His was a smile she had to fight for.

Imani recognized a spark of something that might have been excitement. Or maybe she was hungry. Either way, she looked forward to next week's session.

FOUR

DESMOND

IN ANOTHER LIFE, Imani would have been a temptation. He would have charmed her, asked her to dinner, put the moves on her...whatever the guys called it these days.

In this life, he knew he had little to offer her. She was a successful analyst who drove a late-model foreign luxury vehicle and probably lived in a high-rise with an elevator and a doorman. He lived in a basement studio apartment, never drove his ten-year-old pickup because the price of gas was so high, and dedicated his life to keeping Bright Pathways running.

No contest.

He sighed, rubbing the back of his neck. He shouldn't even be thinking about her like that. He couldn't afford to get distracted, and once she found out about how he'd spent his early thirties, she wouldn't be interested anyway.

Desmond hiked a backpack onto his shoulder, gave one

last look at the now-darkened community center, and began the walk home. The streets were quiet, save for the occasional car whizzing by. As he approached home, he passed the familiar artwork on the side of the building and the crumbling concrete steps leading up to the front door. Once he keyed into the building, he descended to the four daylight basement studios and unlocked his apartment.

His place was small—a single room with a bed in one corner, a two-seater couch, and a kitchenette. The bathroom was just large enough to hold a sink, tub, and toilet. He'd repaired and painted pocked and hole-filled walls, polished the wood floors, and cleaned the place up as best he could when he first moved in. It wasn't much, but it was his.

Desmond tossed his backpack on the couch and headed to the kitchenette. He opened a cupboard, grabbed two packages of ramen, and set a pot of water to boil on the stove. While waiting, he leaned against the counter and pulled out his phone.

His nightly ritual was to scroll through a list of chat sites, podcasts, and social media. He ended up at Beyond Bars, a support forum for previously incarcerated individuals during re-entry. A video post caught his eye from a new user. He tapped to play, then pulled down a soup bowl from the cabinet and opened the refrigerator.

"Yo, what up, y'all?" said the poster. He sat behind the wheel of a car, the interior dark, he wore a hoodie and sported a few days of beard growth. "I been out a minute. Did a little over three years of a six-year bid. It was some bullshit, but you know, had to see it through. I was in the halfway house for a while, but I'm staying with my moms now. This is where probation is holding me, anyway."

Desmond pulled a few items from the refrigerator to spruce up his ramen—a few slices of link sausage, shallots, spinach, cabbage, and a hard-boiled egg. While his water boiled, he chopped, then sautéed the mixture together while he watched the video.

"The goal is to stay on the straight and narrow, you know? It's hard, though. I came back to my old hood, my old friends, the old business. I got to have a job, bring some money in, but you know how it goes. Nobody wants to hire a felon."

Desmond's heart went out to MrGoodstuff82. He remembered the days after his release. Though his circumstances were different, the struggle to rebuild felt familiar.

"I don't know how long I can hang. My P.O. is breathing down my neck. I got restitution I gotta pay." MrGoodstuff82 looked away, his eyes focused on something in the distance.

"I hear you, brother," Desmond muttered, stirring the meat and vegetables into the noodles, then pouring them into a bowl. The video continued, MrGoodstuff82's tone growing more agitated.

"I'm trying to do right, know what I'm saying? The system, man. It's set up for us to fail. How I'm supposed to do right when I can't even get a job flipping burgers? I paid my debt. I'm just trying to live out here."

Desmond carried his steaming soup and a water bottle to the secondhand coffee table. He set the phone down, propping it against the bottle to watch while he ate. MrGoodstuff82 reminded him of himself before his sentence was overturned and the charges expunged. He'd been lucky to find a role at Bright Pathways, but not everyone had that kind of luck.

He finished his ramen, videos scrolling in the background. Then Desmond went back to MrGoodstuff82's post and opened the comment section.

'Hey MrGoodstuff82, Desmond here. I've been out for a few years after eighteen months down on wire fraud. I know it seems tough, and I hear the frustration in your voice, but you got this, man. You can't win a game you're not playing. Don't give up, don't go back. Have you checked out any re-entry programs or in-person support groups in your area? From the area around you in the car, looks like Atlanta. I'm local— we can try to locate some resources for you. There are employers that will take a chance on a good employee. There are places you can live if things with your mom don't work out.'

He hit send and returned to his dinner. His evenings usually looked like this—dinner, watching videos, posting messages of support to fellow ex-convicts. He might watch a movie, but most of the time, he pulled up YouTube on the Roku device he'd gifted himself for Christmas and watched videos until he couldn't keep his eyes open.

His belly full, Desmond stretched his legs under the table and yawned. Imani came to mind. He wondered how a woman like her spent her evenings.

She probably rushed home to a handsome man in an expensive suit who would be waiting for her at the door. He would present her with a cocktail and lead her to an elegantly set table where something fancy had been prepared for a late meal.

His phone buzzed with a notification. MrGoodstuff82 had replied to his comment.

'Thanks for reaching out, man. Yeah, I'm in Atlanta. Any leads would be appreciated. I'm trying, but it's hard out here.'

Desmond sat up straighter, his fingers flying over the phone's keyboard. 'Atlanta's got some good programs. Check *out the Georgia Justice Project. They've got job training and legal services.'*

He spent the next hour sharing resources, firing off links to job training programs, housing assistance, and support groups in the Atlanta area. As the conversation wound down, Desmond felt drained. He was glad he could help, but the weight of others' struggles sometimes felt heavy on his shoulders, especially since as much as he helped others, there was so little help for him.

Desmond glanced at the clock and sighed. He should've been in bed an hour ago.

He hoped the rest of the week and the weekend passed quickly. He was already looking forward to seeing Imani Thatcher again.

FIVE

IMANI

IMANI AND CASEY made their way through the Dekalb Farmer's market, baskets in hand, chatting as they browsed the stalls filled with fresh produce, artisanal goods, and local crafts. The air carried the scent of freshly baked bread, ripe fruits, and blooming flowers.

"Why are we here again?" Casey asked, eyeing a display of vibrant heirloom tomatoes. "We always do Whole Foods."

"I wanted to pick up a few things," Imani replied, her eyes scanning the stalls. "I haven't cooked in ages, and I thought it might be nice to get some fresh ingredients. It's part of my plan to invest in myself, to get back to things I enjoy—like cooking. I got far too accustomed to going out, being wined and dined. I never used to eat like that before I met Julian."

A manicured eyebrow rose. "You need more than organic tomatoes to get over that man."

Imani chuckled. "I know, but it's a start. I need to do

things that make me happy, that make me feel like myself again. Cooking used to be one of those things."

"Alright, fair enough," Casey conceded. "But if you really want to move on, you need to get out of the house. Meet people, have fun. Not that I don't love you, baby girl, but I can't be the only person you know."

"I know plenty of people. You're just...the only person that doesn't get on my damn nerves. Besides," she said, reaching for a block of fresh mozzarella and placing it in her basket, "I'm going to know plenty of people pretty soon. That pro bono project goes for six weeks. That's six weeks with nosy seventeen-year-olds—"

"And one sexy adult," Casey finished. "What's his deal? You want me to look him up?"

"No, I do not," Imani chided. "I have no reason to know more about that man. I won't know him in six weeks."

In truth, she didn't need any more reasons to think about Desmond. She hadn't been able to stop thinking about him since her session at Bright Pathways. There was something about him—his intensity, his dedication to the kids, the way he carried himself—that intrigued her.

Well, more than intrigued her. She'd had more than one daydream about his firm body pinning her against the hood of her car, then leaning in to graze thick, plump lips against hers.

Her body thumped in response. Imani shook her head, trying to clear the unbidden thoughts.

I can't afford to get tangled up in another complicated situation, especially not with someone involved with my work.

"Earth to Imani," Casey said, waving a hand in front of her face. "Where'd you go just now?"

"Nowhere," she replied quickly.

Casey smirked, clearly unconvinced. "Mmhmm. He got your sin engine rumblin', huh? Well, if you change your mind, let me know. I'm just saying, a little background check never hurt nobody, and it's good to be prepared."

"You're incorrigible. Grab some of those bell peppers; they're a nice size. I'll grab some onions, and maybe some fresh herbs. I'm thinking of making some tomato sauce."

"Don't sauce need to cook all day?"

"Where am I going, Casey? I can put it on when I get home and let it simmer."

As they moved through the market, Imani relaxed. She even hummed a little, finding the simple act of selecting fresh ingredients and planning a meal soothing. It reminded her of quieter times, before the whirlwind of a relationship with a high-energy man had changed her life. This was what she needed—a return to normalcy, to the things that brought her joy.

As they rounded a corner, Imani gasped, eyes widening. A few stalls down, a familiar figure stood looking good enough to eat in a fitted t-shirt and loose jeans. He wore headphones and seemed oblivious to the two women staring. His basket overflowed with white packages from the meat counter and an assortment of vegetables.

"That guy right there—" Imani whispered, tugging on Casey's arm.

"Mmmhmm," said Casey. "That's about what you need." She let out a low, animalistic grunt. "I can't tell what he's packing from here, but those arms look like he knows where the gym is."

"Casey, that's *Desmond!* The guy from the community center."

Casey's mouth dropped open and her eyes grew wide as they ogled his muscles flexing when he reached for a bundle of herbs. "Ohhhh. *Okay*. I see why you won't shut up about him."

"I don't talk about him...a lot." But even as she said it, her gaze remained fixed on Desmond's figure.

"Uh-huh," Casey replied with a knowing smirk. "Go say hello."

"Nope." Imani shook her head, turning around and pulling Casey away before Desmond could see them staring him down. "I just need a few more things and then I am going home."

"You sure?" Casey asked teasingly. "He looks like he cooks. Maybe y'all can make sauce together."

"Shut up and come on here," Imani insisted, leading them out of the section.

But fate had other plans. Desmond was in the same checkout line a few spots ahead of them. Imani's pulse quickened, an unmistakable flutter stirring. She eyed him from behind, then watched him chatting with the clerk as she bagged his groceries. His skin was smooth, his features chiseled. She noticed—again—his lips and how they were naturally slightly parted. Before she could stop it, the same daydream she'd been indulging in for the past few days rolled across her mind.

"If you don't stop staring at that man, he's gonna bust into flame," muttered Casey. She grabbed a magazine and handed it to Imani. "If you're not going to say hi, keep your eyes busy looking at something else."

Desmond must have sensed their presence because he turned suddenly, meeting Imani's gaze. He looked away then back to her, as if he had to double-check that he was seeing who he'd just seen. His expression morphed from confused to surprised and back to confused.

Imani was momentarily frozen, unable to pull her eyes

from his. The clerk said something to him, which was the only reason he tore his stare away.

"Fuck," she muttered under her breath.

"Watch, when we get outside, he'll be waiting."

"Probably. What am I supposed to say?"

"Say hi like a normal person. He won't always be connected to your job."

As Imani and Casey exited the market, they spotted Desmond waiting near the entrance, arms crossed over his chest. His bags sat at his feet.

"Hey," Imani said, trying to keep her voice casual. "I can't believe I ran into you here."

"I was about to say the same thing," said Desmond. "You don't shop here often, do you?"

"Not in years," said Imani, shaking her head. "I used to come here with my mother ages ago. I guess I was in the mood for nostalgia. Do you...shop here?"

"About once a month, yeah. They carry things I can't get at the neighborhood grocery. Once I got used to cooking my own food, it was hard to get into subpar produce and grocery store meat. The prices are better than Whole Foods, too, so I stock up."

"I think those are great money-saving tips," said Imani. "You seem to know the value of a dollar. One might wonder why you have someone come in to teach workshops."

Desmond's easy smile fell like a brick wall. His eyes grew hard, then he glanced away. "I, uh... I just realized I've got an appointment. I need to run. But we'll see you Thursday."

"Sure..." Imani said, drawing out the word. "Was it something I said? I didn't mean to offend—"

"You didn't. I just... I need to go. Great seeing you." He

bent to pick up his bags and walked away, stalking quickly toward a pickup truck.

"Well, damn," Casey said, reminding Imani that she was there. "What crawled up his ass?"

"I don't know," Imani muttered. "I touched a nerve, it seems. I don't know if I want to find out what that's about. I've spent enough time wondering what the hell is going on with men. Let's go. I want to get my sauce on."

SIX

DESMOND

DESMOND LEANED AGAINST THE WINDOWSILL, a knot of anxiety twisting in his stomach as he scanned the parking lot. As predicted, Imani's car pulled into its usual spot, parked where she could keep an eye on it at all times.

The memory of their brief encounter at the farmers' market had replayed again and again in his mind. He had not handled it well; his past made him guarded and defensive.

Desmond watched Imani climb out of her car and push the door closed. She hiked a bag on her shoulder, dressed this time in a dark, well-cut pantsuit, a silky blouse that clung to her shape, and heels that accentuated the cut and color of her suit.

Damn. It had been a minute since he'd been with a woman, even before his stint at Jesup, a minimum-security prison camp. He'd been so buried in work that he hadn't even noticed that he was being framed, then targeted and investigated. Dating, romance, and anything of the sort had become a low priority.

Now, though? With a free and clear name, with the new path he was forging, with his efforts to give back and heal as much as he could? Things could be different.

Yeah, right, he mumbled to himself. A woman like Imani would never consider him an option.

She crossed the parking lot, her long legs striding confidently across the pavement. A few minutes later, Imani appeared in the doorway of the lounge. She offered him a tight smile as she paused at the threshold. Desmond nodded in acknowledgment, then waved her inside.

"Okay, pantsuit! Go 'head, heels!" Deja shouted.

The tension in her face melted as she burst into laughter. "Hello, Deja. I will admit I got dressed this morning wondering if you would have something to say."

"I like seeing your fashions. It's kind of inspirational."

"You sound like you might want to go into fashion and merchandising. Any interest?"

Deja shrugged, pulling at the bright pink hoodie she wore over jeans and pristine sneakers. "Maybe. I don't know how to get that kind of job."

"Well, we can talk about it."

"Alright, guys," said Desmond, his voice rising to cut through the hum of noise. "Huddle up for today's session with Ms. Imani. Try not to waste her time this week."

He tipped his head in her direction and stepped aside as the group settled into their seats.

Imani set her bag down on a chair and moved to the front of the room. "Thank you, Desmond. So, last week, y'all were real nosy about my finances, so I'm about to get into your business. Who here knows what a budget is?"

Caleb raised his hand, a mischievous grin on his lips.

"That's when you're broke and can't afford anything fun, so you gotta count every penny."

The room erupted in laughter, and Imani chuckled. "Close, Caleb. That's certainly one approach. A budget is a plan that helps you allocate your income to cover your expenses and save for the future. Let's start by talking about the different categories of expenses. Tell me what you spend your money on, and I'll tell you where they fall."

"Food!" shouted one. Imani glanced at Desmond. He picked up the hint and grabbed a dry-erase marker to note the responses.

"Clothes!" added another.

"Loud," chimed in a third. The room tittered in laughter, snickers, and hand slaps.

"Loud?" Imani repeated.

"Uhm...weed," Desmond muttered, just loud enough for her to hear.

She frowned, confused. "Why do they call it—anyway. Loud. Weed. Bud. Marijuana. Got it. What else?"

Deja, slouched comfortably in the couch, noted, "I'll tell you what I'm not buying is those shoes. I know they cost a whole paycheck."

Imani smiled, glancing down at her heels. "The point of this exercise is to prioritize your needs—things you absolutely must have to survive, like food, shelter, and clothing—over your wants, like designer fashion. Or video games...or *loud*."

The teens murmured amongst themselves about budgetary priorities and whether weed came before food, shelter, and clothing.

"Now we'll talk about income," Imani continued. "That's the money you earn from your job, allowance, or any other source. You need to know how much money you're bringing in each month so you can plan your budget accordingly. Money is what we call a finite resource. Once it's gone, it's gone."

She turned to the whiteboard, picked up another marker, and wrote out a simple equation. "The basic formula for creating a budget is income minus expenses. What's left is for savings and what I call discretionary or... fun money."

Caleb raised his hand again. "What if there's nothing left to save? What if your expenses are higher than your income? You supposed to never have fun?"

Imani nodded, appreciating the question. "Those are valid questions, Caleb. If you find that your expenses are greater than your income, you have to adjust your spending or increase your income. This is where a side gig or additional work might come in handy. I'm talking overtime at work, mowing lawns, babysitting. I'm talking a legit source of income, not anything nefarious, and don't insult me by pretending you don't know what I mean."

"She talking to you, Caesar," said Caleb.

"Man, shut up talkin' about my business."

"Alright, alright. This is a safe space—no snitching in here. Let's talk bank accounts super quickly because before you start earning and saving, you need a place to put the money, right? Most of you will be eighteen in a few months and can open your own accounts. Let's make sure you know what to look for."

The teens listened intently, their faces masks of varying degrees of interest as Imani explained the different types of bank accounts, fees, and interest rates.

As the session came to a close, Desmond stepped forward, rubbing his palms together.

"You guys did great, and so did Ms. Imani. I hope you

got good information that you can use. Don't forget the homework—come next week with three credit unions, right?" Desmond held up three fingers in the air. "Caesar, what are we looking for?"

"Requirements for opening an account, if they offer interest-bearing checking accounts, and...what interest rate they pay?"

"Gold star!" said Imani, packing up her bag.

As the group dispersed and voices faded, Desmond began tidying up the room. He rearranged the tables and chairs, putting the couches back in their usual layout. When he turned around, he realized he was alone with Imani. He'd assumed that she had left with the group, but she was still there, leaning against the desk in the corner. The air between them crackled with an intense, almost tangible tension. The elephant in the room was now a raging bull.

"This must be where you work," said Imani quietly.

Desmond nodded, picking up items as he slowly made his way to the front. "This space used to be an office and a conference room. There was nowhere for the older kids to hang out, so I knocked down the wall, pulled up the carpet, picked up some secondhand furniture, added the whiteboards."

He angled his thumb toward the two whiteboards hung on the wall at the head of the room. "The foosball, pool, and paddle ball tables were donated. They really brightened the spot up. Plus it gives them a place to be when it's too cold for basketball outside."

"These children—young adults, really—are incredibly fortunate to have this place. And you. I can't imagine if every teenager on the cusp of adulthood had someone that cared about how they entered the world the way you do."

"It keeps the kids off the street, and for that, the mayor is grateful. So long as we keep up on grants from the state and annual donations, we do alright."

"I see." The silence stretched out, heavy and expectant, before Imani let out a deep sigh and stood. "Well, tonight's session went long. I apologize for keeping you here late—"

"Imani, hold up," Desmond interrupted. "I need to apologize for my behavior at the farmers' market. I was rude. You didn't do anything wrong, you didn't say anything wrong. It's totally a me thing and it wasn't fair to treat you that way."

Imani's eyes glowed in surprise. "I had wondered, so thank you. I get it. Everyone is fighting their own battle, including me." After a moment, she laced her fingers together and continued. "You know, this is absolutely outside my purview as a person that's just here offering a workshop to your center, but I'm not just here for them; I'm here for you, too. If there's something on your mind, I have ears. Sometimes it helps to talk it out."

Desmond paused for a long moment, warring inside himself. He didn't make a habit of sharing his feelings, revealing his past. People treated him differently once they found out about his prison stint. Most of them didn't wait to find out how the experience had changed him, how he was still damaged, how he'd cleared his name. He wondered if he could trust Imani to listen and understand.

There was only one way to find out. If things went badly, he only had to stick it out for four more weeks.

"Could I buy you a drink from the vending machine?" he asked. "We can sit and talk if you have a minute."

Imani nodded, beaming a warm smile. "I'd like that."

He rose from his seat and left, returning with two ice-cold bottles of cola, condensation dripping down the sides. Alongside them were two packs of crackers and cheese.

"These things are addictive," Desmond said, handing her a bottle and a pack of crackers. "I went a long time not having anything like this. Now I have them every day."

They settled on the worn couches in the lounge, quietly munching. Imani seemed content to wait until he was ready to open up.

"So, I've been running this place for the past few years. It's not really what I set out to do with my life, but circumstances have made it so I kind of have to take what I can get. Bright Pathways works because I make it work, but there's a lot on my shoulders here. There's so much I could do if I had more money, more time, more resources. But there's something else holding me back. I'm reminded of it every day, and it's a big reason why I don't run these workshops for the kids. I just... I really just need you to listen and not judge. There's a full story I want to share."

"Ears open, judgment off," she replied, then popped the last of a cheddar cheese and peanut butter cracker into her mouth.

He hesitated, setting down his bottle of cola. "There's not an easy, gentle way to say this, but...I'm about five years out of prison."

He heard her suck in a quiet breath and lean back slightly. When he had worked up enough courage, his eyes rose to find hers searching his face as if trying to reconcile the man she thought she knew with the one he was revealing.

"I spent a couple years in a federal prison camp for embezzlement and wire fraud, though it's more involved than that. Since I got out, I've been trying to make a life for myself."

Desmond watched her reaction, his heart growing heavy as he saw the shock sink in. He braced himself for what was to come: the judgment she said she had turned off but would surely surface, followed by the distance, the cold politeness, and the curt completion of her project before she simply faded away.

In that moment, though, he'd done something he rarely did anymore: shared a deep, hidden piece of himself that was a large part of his life. He spoke his truth and now he had to let it settle between them.

SEVEN

IMANI

WELL. That was unexpected.

Though given her recent track record with men, she was not surprised. Of course, a man that she was fighting an attraction to had a dark past.

After a few moments of silence and *did I hear what I think I heard?* rapid eye-blinks, Imani leaned in, reached out a hand and placed it on his arm, her grip warm and reassuring.

"Thank you for trusting me with that. How is there... *more* to embezzlement and wire fraud?"

Desmond paused for a beat. He had probably expected her to gather her designer purse, get into her luxury vehicle, and tear out of the parking lot. Instead, she leaned in close like some sort of emotional leech, thirsty for lurid details of a tarnished past.

"I was working for a construction company, managing the business office. Writing bids, booking jobs, scheduling the crews. They needed some extra help and my mom talked me into asking them to hire my brother. Shawn is..."

He paused to push a puff of irritated breath from his nose. "He's smart in all the wrong ways. Like...dumb as hell, but he can crack a safe, you know? He'd been in and out of jail in his youth for petty shit, but his record was sealed when he turned eighteen and he'd put on this act like he was on the straight and narrow, he just needed a good job to hold him down. So..."

Desmond splayed his hands in a helpless gesture. "I talked my bosses into hiring him to help out at the office. Nothing heavy, do up some invoices, send them out. When the payments came in, I made the deposits, but he'd reconcile the accounts."

"I don't think I like where this is going."

"Yeah," he said, nodding. "I didn't like it either when an audit uncovered discrepancies in the accounts. Money was missing, things weren't lining up. They launched a quiet investigation and turned up all kinds of evidence that traced back to transactions made under my login. I was none the wiser because I had no idea what had been happening behind my back."

"Shawn."

Again, he nodded. "Shawn would manipulate the invoices I'd given him to reconcile, then used my login credentials to skim the overage to a separate account. At the first whiff that they'd found out about it, Shawn disappeared. Their investigator dug up his expunged record. There was no way I could prove it wasn't me. And even if I could, was I taking my brother down?"

"So you took the charge."

He nodded. "My parents mortgaged the house, whatever they had to pay for a lawyer. I ended up taking a deal and getting twenty-four months."

Desmond paused, running a palm over his low-cut hair, then pulling his fingers through his beard. "I was sentenced to Jesup Prison Camp about four hours south, so my mom could visit. She has COPD, so she can't really travel. If you're going to do time and the offense isn't violent, a camp isn't all that bad.

"Halfway through my sentence, Shawn popped up. The guilt must have been eating him up and he could never keep a secret. It got around that he had confessed to committing the crimes under my name. My lawyer petitioned for my release based on his statement and they let me out on supervised release. My record was cleared after Shawn's trial, but the damage had been done."

Imani reached out, gently squeezing his hand. "That must have been incredibly difficult."

Desmond shrugged, not meeting her lingering stare. "Serving the time wasn't half as bad as being free but still having to report to a babysitter and having a curfew. I'd do all of my time if it meant I didn't have to hear my mother raging at me for putting her baby boy in prison. She said I was already halfway through the sentence and Shawn could have made it up to me after I was out."

"It's been years now. Is your mom still upset?"

"We don't talk—me and my mom, me and Shawn." He shook his head. "There's nothing...*nothing* I want from him. I don't have anything to say to either of them."

"And what happened to Shawn?"

"He did some time and was released early. Now he's out in the world with a felony on his record. He could have had a real good job, you know?"

He pushed out a heavy breath, then rubbed a thumb

across his bottom lip as if deep in thought. "My father had a heart attack during all of this and was forced to retire. My folks split up. He's the only one I talk to. That old man has been by my side through everything."

Imani hung on his every word. She felt his determination and inner strength, seeing his drive to overcome the past and make a difference. She squeezed his hand again.

"So you don't teach classes on money management because you went to prison for money crimes?"

"Correct," he replied with a deep nod. "It's about the appearance of things. I don't ever want anything to come back on these kids. I need to be above reproach at all times."

"But... it wasn't *you* that did the crime. And you were exonerated after Shawn confessed—"

"Most people aren't going to get that far if they look me up. They'll see the felony but not the exoneration. They'll see the prison time but not the years I've spent rehabbing this shitty building someone signed over to the city and making it a safe space for these kids. I don't want to see that look in their eyes, like they're wondering if I'm on some con. Or worse, running a racket out of here. I ain't that dude."

"I hate this for you, Desmond. It's not fair."

He lifted and lowered his shoulders in a shrug, as if he had long ago come to terms with the injustice of it all. "Life isn't fair. I tell these kids that every day. You have to find a way to keep it moving."

"I believe you. It's still not fair." Imani paused for a breath, just to take everything in. Then she perked up, gazing at Desmond sort of sideways.

"You have a question about prison," he said, almost smiling. "I see it on your face."

"Forgive me. I'm... I suddenly have a hundred questions."

He sighed, but not heavily. "What do you want to know?"

"Just...we were both at the Farmers Market, and I noticed you had a lot of fresh vegetables in your cart. I've been trying to get back into cooking, and I was thinking about what it must be like to cook and eat in prison, then to get out and be in charge of your own food. I guess having fresh food must mean a lot to you."

"Fresh, *good* food. Yeah, I like to cook. Even the regular grocery store produce doesn't compare to what I can get fresh. I try to hit the Farmers Market every few weeks."

"You must have something you still eat, even though you're not in prison. Sort of like how my grandparents still eat pigs' feet even though we've been free and we don't have to eat that anymore."

Desmond pretended to retch, rolling his eyes. "No pig feet, but uh..." He chuckled, rubbing a few fingers over his lips before answering. "Like these crackers, I grew a taste for ramen noodles. Not the fancy Japanese style noodles but the cheap ten-cents-a-pack stuff."

"Desmond..." Imani shook her head. "Oh, honey, no...."

"Aye, look—you gotta fix it up. Dice up some meat, vegetables, sauté it up with seasoning and something to give it a little kick, then add an egg and let it cook. You want your noodles slightly al dente. Sometimes I pan-fry some dumplings and have those on the side with soy sauce. Don't knock it 'til you try it."

Imani laughed. "I don't know if I want to try that."

"Fine," he said, sucking his teeth. "Be bougie about it. You're missing out."

"I don't think so, Desmond."

Imani was in trouble.

Desmond had just spilled his deep, dark past as a felon,

a former inmate at a prison camp, and she hadn't found a reason to get up and rush out, never to darken the doors of Bright Pathways ever again.

On the contrary, she admired the way he had turned his life around, the way he was using his experiences to make a difference.

Maybe some of that could rub off on me.

"I need to get you out of here," said Desmond after a while. "It's way too late for your car to be on this side of town."

He snapped off lights, closed doors, and locked the front doors on the way out. The sky was pitch black, the lot was empty, and the crickets and cicadas were creating a chorus. Imani unlocked her car, then turned to face Desmond.

"I don't want to get all...*goopy*...but I do want to thank you for telling your story, for trusting me with your feelings and experiences. It means a lot to me, and frankly...I needed a shock of reality."

Desmond tipped his head, allowing a small smile to bend his lips. "Anytime you need a dose of reality, I'm here. I'm glad you stayed."

Desmond waited until she got into her car, started the engine, and pulled out of her spot to step back and offer a wave.

As she merged onto the highway, she called out to the Bluetooth system. "Call Casey!"

She answered on the second ring. "Girl, where the hell you been? I thought you only had to be out there for two hours. I was about to call the police."

Imani laughed. "To do what? Mosey on down below I-20 whenever they feel like it to check out a missing Black woman?"

"You have a point. So you're alive."

"I am. And girl! There is a development with Desmond."

"Like I need to come over with Chunky Monkey and rosé kind of development?"

"No, this can't wait. And you're going to wish you'd found this out before me. Desmond is a felon. About five years out of a prison camp."

Casey's chuckle rolled around low in her throat before bursting across the line. "You sure know how to pick 'em, 'Mani. So that's where you've been? Listening to a felon give you his sob story?"

"He told me everything. Look him up—him and his brother Shawn. His brother actually committed the crime under his name. Desmond went to prison, then Shawn popped back up, and looks like they just switched prisoners. Now they're both out, but he doesn't talk to Shawn."

"I'm concerned that you don't sound sufficiently alarmed by this information."

"White-collar, not violent. Look him up."

"Alright, alright. What is his name?"

"Desmond Taylor. Look up, uhmmmm... He said Jesup Prison Camp. And Shawn. Stuff should pop up."

Casey was silent for a moment, save the sound of keys tapping. "Okay, I found an article. Something about him being released due to new evidence that exonerates him..."

More keys tapping.

"Yep. 'Defendant Desmond Taylor served just under three years for wire fraud when it was discovered that the defendant's brother, Shawn, committed the crime and framed him. Mr. Taylor's sentence was reduced and he was discharged on supervised release pending a hearing.' And it's a mugshot of him looking sad but all kinds of swarthy. Lookin' real prison jacked."

"Right..."

"Imani...now—"

"Casey, just hold on." Imani sighed. "We had a long, heartfelt talk. I can tell he's a good man. He's been through a lot, but he's taking this second chance seriously. The kids really like him, and you know how teenagers can be."

"If nobody will tell you about yourself, a teenager will. I guess that's one mark in his corner."

"And you did tell me I have to find a way to get over Julian. There's no better way to get over somebody than—"

"I did not tell you go get up under the first man you come across, let alone an ex-con."

"Technically, he's not an ex-con. His conviction was overturned; he's free and clear."

Casey huffed. "Why you always gotta go for a handsome man with a past? So what you finna do? I thought you couldn't be involved with him while you're doing the workshops."

"I shouldn't. I don't even know if he's interested, to be honest."

"Imani Thatcher, Ima jump through this phone. A few weeks ago you had a man hiding a whole wife and family to come to Atlanta and break multiple things, including your headboard and your back. Acting like Desmond might not be interested in your fine ass is gonna piss me off."

Imani burst into laughter. "You are too good for my ego, old woman. Go to bed. We'll talk tomorrow."

"I ain't going to bed. I'm going to put together a little dossier before you see Mr. Felon next week. We're going into this one with our eyes wide open."

"Do not call that man Mr. Felon."

"*Mmmph.* Item number one—think of a cute name for Mr. Felon since Imani don't like that name."

"I can't stand you. Goodnight."

"For real, Imani. Guard your heart. You know I'm always here for you, no matter what."

She smiled, grateful for her friend's constant support and available shoulder. "I know, Casey. Love you, girl. Thank you."

EIGHT

DESMOND

THE HARSH BUZZ of the alarm shattered the quietness of the pre-dawn hours, but Desmond hadn't needed an alarm in years.

Before prison, a career in construction meant he was in the office before most of the staff, so he'd be organized when people started showing up. At Jesup, every morning began at 5 AM. His bed was made, living quarters organized, and daily chapters read in his latest library book before the duty officer came to collect his dorm mates for showers, exercise, and breakfast. Then it would be time for enrichment—classes, counseling or community service, and a shift in maintenance or welding.

Day in and day out, it was the same routine, making the months fly by mostly. He only knew what day it was because every other Thursday, his parents came for visitation, and toward the end, his lawyer was dropping by often.

After his release, he found comfort in the routine. Each

morning followed the same pattern—up at 5 AM, a run to the neighborhood 24-hour gym, a workout that pushed his body to remember discipline, then run home for a shower, breakfast, reading and journaling, then daily posts on Beyond Bars. Depending on the day, he would then head to Bright Pathways for work.

The center was only open for a few hours a day on the weekend, but the part-time staff were on shift and could handle it. He tried to take the weekends to decompress so he would be fresh for the kids that would come through the doors throughout the week.

By early afternoon, he had washed and dried a bag of laundry. Since he wasn't hungry yet, he pulled on a pair of basketball shoes and hopped into his pickup, headed for the outdoor courts at Bessie Branham Park. The distinct red and black courts were a state-of-the-art design by the Atlanta Hawks and a popular place to play.

The usual crowd milled around. Sweat glistened on players' skin, a testament to the day's heat. The thump of bass from a nearby car stereo rumbled. Desmond laced up and started a warm-up game by himself. Soon he was lost in the rhythmic swish of the ball going through the net.

After about thirty minutes, he was recruited to join a pick-up game. The exertion helped to clear his mind, give him something to focus on. He was crouched in deep concentration, watching a player about to take a shot, when a familiar silhouette caught his eye.

Desmond straightened, his attention drawn to the person walking along the fence surrounding the court. He signaled for a substitute player, giving them a fist bump in gratitude before stepping off the court and heading toward the fence.

"The fuck you doing here, Shawn?" he spat out, his

words venomous. "Nothing's changed since the last time you tried to pull this brother-to-brother bullshit."

Shawn nonchalantly shrugged, his hands buried in his pockets. The casual gesture only intensified Desmond's simmering anger. "I don't need a reason to check up on my big brother."

"You didn't check up on your big brother when I was doing your time in Jesup."

Desmond could have predicted the irritated eye roll that came. "Here we go with the martyr speech, like Jesup was Rikers or Folsom. You was literally at a camp serving white-collar time."

"*Your* time. Time you should have been serving because you implicated me and then dipped. It doesn't matter how much time I served or where I served it; it was supposed to be *yours*."

"You say that like I ain't do time too."

Desmond's upper lip twisted; he fought to keep his tightly gripped fists at his sides as he struggled to control his emotions. "You did a year, Shawn. After I served twice that before you showed up to take accountability. And had to be forced to do that."

"Look, man. As fun as it is to spar with you or whatever, I needed to find you because Mom's not doing well. You need to roll by the house. Soon."

Shawn's words felt like he'd been punched in the chest. He hadn't kept in touch with his mother, and the news of her worsening health hit hard.

"Where'd you hear that?" he asked. "Dad didn't say anything about her being sick."

Shawn folded his arms, averting his eyes as if he was casing the basketball courts. "Just passing along the message. She's been asking about you. Thought you should know."

Desmond stared at Shawn. "Thanks for the message," he replied finally, then walked back to the basketball game.

The damage, however, was done. His mind was already elsewhere. He played mechanically; his shots were off, his passes sloppy. He had no concentration or heart in the game. After a few minutes of effort, he snatched up his bag and headed back to his pickup.

He arrived at his apartment visibly agitated. There were reasons he didn't see his family, especially those that weren't supportive of him while he was inside or after he'd come out. Now his energy was off, his routine was threatened, and he wasn't sure how to get himself back on the right path.

Desmond picked up his phone, looking for a distraction on Beyond Bars, but was scrolling through posts, not really reading them. An alert from Instagram popped up on his phone.

_im_thatcher has sent you a private message._

He squinted, his brows nearly knit together. Imani sent him an Instagram DM?

Without hesitation, he swiped the notification, opening the app to his direct messages.

'I'm not stalking you, I swear. My phone must have pinged from the area because you're showing up as someone I should follow. Weird, huh?'

He didn't know whether to laugh or be creeped out by this coincidence.

'Yeah, that's weird how phones do that. What's up. How is your Saturday?'

'Pretty good," she wrote back. *Deep cleaned my place, went to yoga. I dropped by the farmers' market again but I*

guess I wouldn't be lucky enough to see you two weekends in a row.'

Was Imani flirting? Or just being friendly? Were women ever just friendly? If she wasn't interested, she'd never have reached out, right? She'd keep things strictly business. So...was she flirting?

'Anyway, sorry if I am disturbing your weekend. I'm about to hit the Chick-a-Biddy close to your side of town, though. I thought you might want to meet up.'

She. Is. Flirting. Fuck.

Desmond was starving. The oatmeal he'd eaten that morning was long burned off. Running into Shawn had decimated his appetite, but the conversation with Imani had reduced his stress...and he could eat.

'You wear Jimmy Choos to work but eat at a low-key neighborhood chicken joint?'

'Don't make me have to prove I'm not bougie, Mr. Taylor. I like chicken. I'm leaving my place now. If you're coming, I'll see you in about a half hour. If not, I'll see you Thursday.'

Desmond stared at his phone for a full sixty seconds, then got up and headed for his shower kit—another habit from prison. His studio included a full bathroom but he kept everything in a caddy. You never knew when you were being moved to another unit or another facility. Desmond was always prepared.

'About to hit the shower. See you in a few.'

Desmond quickly showered, lined up his beard and his hairline while he was at it, slathered on lotion and threw on a t-shirt and jeans, then grabbed his keys and headed out. He pulled up to Chick-a-Biddy, parked next to Imani's BMW in the lot, and walked in, spotting her immediately at a table in a sunny corner wearing a pair of oversized sunglasses. She wore a fitted Prince t-shirt and understated jewelry. Her hair, which was normally in a subdued style, was a halo of loose curls and twists around her face. He found he liked it, but he tried not to stare too long.

"You made it," she said, sliding a menu over for him to peruse.

"Almost didn't recognize you without your suit on," he said, sliding into the booth opposite her.

Imani laughed, removing her sunglasses and setting them down on the table. "I have layers, Desmond."

"Yeah, yeah. Lemme see what shoes you got on." He bent to peer at the rest of her outfit, smiling at the cut of her tailored leather shorts and impeccable, spotless leather and suede sneakers. "You're not beating the bougie charges, Imani."

"I can't help that I like nice clothes. You're not looking bad, Mr. Has To Take A Shower To Eat Chicken."

"I worked out, did some laundry. I had actually just got home from playing ball..." The conversation with Shawn flashed across his mind, putting a brief damper on his mood.

"Let's order," Imani suggested. "And then we can both talk about what just happened to your face."

Nearly an hour later, they picked at the remnants of fried chicken, spicy collard greens, and an order of sweet potato fries to share. Imani had talked around a few issues on her mind—boredom at work, feeling aimless with her life and harboring a desire to restart, and the recent death of a friend.

Desmond got the idea that this man was much more than a friend. It stirred feelings of envy within him—feelings he had no right to allow to fester.

"I thought going to the funeral would give me the

closure I needed. And I am better, but...I think about him a lot."

"It's probably going to take more than a few weeks to come to terms. Maybe closure isn't what you really need. I don't think any of us really need closure."

"Oh?" Imani bit off half of the last sweet potato fry. "What do we really need?"

Desmond shrugged a bulky shoulder, crossing his arms and leaning forward onto the table. "Healing, honestly. I know I do."

"What are you working on healing from? You seem like someone with a lot going around in your head."

"I do?" When Imani confirmed with a nod, he gave the notion a second thought. "I mean, you're not wrong. There is a lot going on in there. And maybe I've been looking for one thing when what I really need is something else. All I want is to put my past behind me. What I really need is to confront it. Confront the people, face the memories. Heal from it so I can move on."

"Mmmm. That's deep, bro. So what does that mean for you? And please know that I'm not trying to be nosy, but if you need to vent, I'm here."

Desmond unfolded his arms and reached for the cup of lemonade, sucking down a few swallows.

"I saw my brother today," he finally confessed. "And it's got me all kinds of fucked up. The way seeing Shawn always has me all kinds of fucked up."

Imani's eyes grew wide. "You've seen him since he got out?"

"Oh, yeah. If it were up to Shawn, we'd be best buds. Especially since we now share the experience of..." Desmond lowered his voice, looking around at the tables surrounding them. No one seemed to be paying attention.

"Being *away*," he finished. "He really thinks we can just go back to how things were before everything blew up. I remember feeling so proud of him. He was doing great at the job. Why couldn't he just...do right? And why did he wrap me up in it? And I'm supposed to just—"

Desmond's fists clenched. He sucked in a breath, feeling himself heading back down the path he'd gone down earlier—enough fury to throw him off for the day. He had to find a way to remove the power and the hold that Shawn had over him.

"He says he found me to tell me that my mom isn't doing well. She's been sick for a while. Thing is, I keep in touch with my Dad. They haven't been together for years, but he still takes care of her. He would pick her up and bring her to see me. Then he would take her to see Shawn when he could, until they shipped him out of state."

"And you don't see her at all?"

Desmond shook his head. "Nah. Last time I saw her was when Shawn was going in. She was so angry with me. She didn't seem happy that I was free. She was mad about Shawn."

He frowned. "Told me everything I needed to know."

"That's sad," Imani said, her lips in a downturn. "In light of what Shawn said, though...do you plan to see her?"

"I don't know. Lord knows what she'll say to me if she thinks it's the last time we'll speak. It could be an apology for how she's treated me, or every name she ever wanted to call me but hasn't been able to."

"That is...certainly something to heal from. You're very much a thinker, Desmond. I admire that."

"It comes from years of having nothing but time to think. If it makes you feel better, a lot of my thoughts are Wu-Tang Clan lyrics. If you like, I'll rap you a verse."

Imani balled up a napkin and threw it at him, chuckling.

"Sometimes I think about shit like...can we ever really trust planes? And when did pineapple on pizza become a thing?"

She laughed hard then, tossing her head back so far he could count all of her pearly white teeth.

Desmond pushed out a long, heavy breath in relief. While it felt amazing to spill his inner thoughts and feelings, finally put air and sounds behind them and let them form words for others to hear, it was simply not fair to dump all over a woman he'd just met. A woman who, though she had certainly been flirting with him, had no idea what she was walking into.

"What you about to do with the rest of your night?" Desmond asked.

Imani frowned. "That question always makes me feel like the asker wants the askee to know their evening plans will not converge."

He tilted his head. "Huh?"

"Like...you just had sex with a young lady, right? Gave her sixteen hot pumps, got the sin engine rumbling as my friend Casey puts it. Then after she collapses in a post-coital heap, you ask her... 'So, what you about to do?' That question means get your shit 'cause you getting put out."

Desmond struggled to maintain his composure as he listened to her explanation, avoiding the temptation to stare at her full lips. The mere thought of giving anyone pumps would set off a chain reaction he couldn't hide for long.

"The fuck kinda dudes you been foolin' with? I just wanted to know if you were ready to head home or if you wanted to hang."

An evil chortle rolled from her. "I want to hang. What are your plans?"

"I like to lay low, to be real. I planned on folding my laundry and watching a movie."

"Fold laundry? Like with your hands?"

"What...nah. Don't tell me you send yours out." Desmond's eyes rolled when she burst into laughter. "Wow. You keep saying you're not bougie, and yet..."

"Don't be like that. I don't mind throwing money at things so they get done. The clothes would sit in the laundry basket for days if I didn't have laundry service."

"I ain't say shit."

"You said I was bougie. So, do you want company while you fold clothes?"

"I wouldn't mind. But you got to be real cool about a few things. I don't have a fancy place or a shiny BMW or designer clothes. I don't have laundry service. I live in a small space that's clean, comfortable, and just enough."

"And you eat ramen."

"You can't talk about my ramen until you taste it."

"Fine, fine. I am real cool about all of those things. And I am ready to get out of this restaurant because I am sure my hair smells like chicken."

Desmond was tempted to offer to be the judge of that but decided against it. Instead, he stacked their empty trays and cups, slid out of the booth and left them at the counter, then pushed the door open and waited for her to exit ahead of him.

"Follow me," he said, slipping a pair of shades over his eyes. "I don't like police, especially in this county, so I don't drive wild. I'd advise you the same." He paused to rake his eyes over her car, then her as she stood at her driver's side door.

He noted her toned thighs and shapely calves. The way her tight t-shirt hugged her didn't escape his notice either, particularly the roundness of her breasts and the curves of her behind. "Especially when you look like that, driving that car."

"They won't like me driving a luxury vehicle while being a fine ass Black woman?"

"Not a bit," Desmond replied, then ducked into his truck and started it up.

NINE

IMANI

IMANI FOLLOWED Desmond's pickup truck through the winding streets of southwest Atlanta, her eyes taking in the unique charm of the neighborhoods. The historic homes, vibrant street art, and lively local businesses gave the area a distinct character that set it apart from the modern, busy architecture of Midtown.

Now you know you don't have no business going to any man's house, let alone this man, she lectured herself. But her curiosity and desire for a new experience overpowered her better judgment. If she was being honest, feeling lonely, missing Julian, and letting Casey convince her that there was no way Desmond wasn't attracted to her fueled her motives just as much.

Desmond parked in a reserved spot; Imani found a space nearby. She grabbed her bag and stepped out of her car, looking around with interest as Desmond approached her.

"It's not much, but it's mine," he said, nodding toward the building.

Imani smiled, appreciating the pride in his voice. "I'm sure it's lovely."

He led her down a flight of stairs to the lower level of the building, unlocked the door, and gestured for her to enter first. Desmond had said his place was 'just enough,' and he was right. It was a cozy room sectioned off into three areas—sleeping area, living space, and kitchen.

The living room held a comfortable-looking couch, a coffee table, and a five-drawer bureau upon which sat a large screen television, a few media devices, and a game console. His style seemed simple but not as utilitarian as she might have expected. A compact kitchenette was tucked into a corner at one end and a bed took up the space at the other side.

On the walls were posters of classic Black films, photos that Imani assumed were friends and loved ones, and a rolling cart stuffed with an impressive number of books. She was immediately drawn to them, her fingers tracing the spines as she scanned the titles ranging from fiction to non-fiction, with a particular emphasis on prison culture, criminal justice, and re-entry.

"Make yourself comfortable," Desmond said, closing the door behind them. "Something to drink? I only keep water and booze in here, but there's a vending machine upstairs. I could get you a Coke or something."

"Oh, water is fine, thanks," Imani replied, setting her bag down on the coffee table. She took a seat on the couch, sinking into the cushions with a contented sigh.

Desmond returned with two bottles of water and handed one to her. He sat down beside her, leaving a respectable amount of space between them. Imani twisted the cap off her bottle and took a sip, her eyes meeting Desmond's.

"What were you planning to watch?"

Desmond grabbed a remote and turned on the TV. The purple Roku screen was already up. "I was thinking something funny. Have you seen *Fight Night*? With Kevin Hart?"

"I haven't, but I'm game," Imani replied. "What's your favorite comedy?"

Desmond thought for a moment before responding. "Too many to name. I like the older movies, you know—*Boomerang. Life. Don't Be A Menace.* I like those Wayans Brothers joints a lot. Back at Jesup, we could do movie nights. They hated when I got to pick because we was always watching *Coming to America* or *Bad Boys*, something like that."

Imani pondered this, tilting her head. "I guess I don't picture you as a guy real big on comedy."

He peered at her, contemplating her comment for a moment. "Sometimes it's a thing where you gotta get some emotion out. You know what I'm saying? You have to emote *something*. Might as well laugh 'cause fuck if I'd be caught crying up in there."

"Aw. It's okay to cry, though."

"Now it is."

He punched a button on the remote and navigated to a menu, then brought up the limited series on a streaming channel. When the opening credits began, he stood. "My laundry is in the truck. You gotta move your bag because I use the table. You plan on helping me fold?"

Imani chortled. "With my hands?"

"I'll work the bougie out of you yet, Imani."

Desmond left and returned a few minutes later with

two duffel bags. He set one of them at Imani's feet and zipped open the other one.

"I would normally just dump these on the couch and go at it, but I'll be a gracious host this time."

"Why, thank you," she said, zipping open the bag at her feet. "I don't have to touch your tighty-whities, do I?"

"Nah, I got the bag with the unmentionables," said Desmond, quickly folding t-shirts with retail-like precision and stacking them on the table. "No telling what you'd do to my boxer briefs. Might take them home with you."

"Don't nobody want your underwear, Desmond."

Imani reached into the bag and pulled out a pair of cotton lounge pants, folded them like a pro, and laid them on the table. Desmond's brows rose.

"*Mmmhmmm.* I used to work at Old Navy. Even when my clothes come back from the laundry service, I refold them before I put them away."

"Oooh... I'm scared o' you, Ms. Thatcher."

"Watch me cook, Mr. Taylor."

They made quick work of both bags while watching the movie and talking, tossing barbs back and forth. Imani took every opportunity to steal glances at Desmond, admiring his strong profile and the way his eyes crinkled at the corners when he laughed. She felt a comfort and ease that was unexpected but not at all unwelcome.

Once the laundry was done and stowed away, Desmond grabbed two glasses and poured them each a shot from a bottle that he unearthed from the kitchen.

"I don't know if you like brown, but...cheers," he said, holding his glass out to her.

"To?" She grabbed the shot glass and sniffed. She smiled at the oak, apple, and orange-tinged aroma of a well-aged bourbon. It reminded her of her dad.

"To meeting new people, I guess. And laundry races." They clinked glasses and downed the amber liquid in one go. Imani coughed as the burn traveled down her throat and through her chest.

"Whoo!" she exclaimed, setting down the empty glass. "That stuff could set something on fire."

"It's not for the faint of heart," Desmond chuckled, adding a bit more to her glass. "I got this bottle when my conviction was overturned and I was officially a free man. I only bring it out on special occasions."

"Laundry night counts as a special occasion?"

"Laundry night with a special guest that lets me talk about my time in prison without making it weird? That lets me give her shit without her taking it personal?" He tipped the glass back and drained it of liquid, then slammed it onto the coffee table. "That's a fucking special occasion."

Imani sipped her second shot more slowly. "You don't have to thank me for being normal. Especially since I caught those side-eyes you gave me the first night I came to Bright Pathways."

"You did, huh?" Desmond smiled, his eyes crinkling up again. She noticed that when he really, really smiled, his whole face lit up. "Well, you're here, aren't you? It didn't scare you away."

"I've got thicker skin than you think I do."

"You always telling me I got you fucked up. Ima find out, I'm sure. But let me ask you something..."

Imani finished her shot and set her glass next to his, then turned so she faced him and moved in closer. "Ask away."

"Why are you here? What was the deal with asking me to eat with you, then making sure you got invited over here?"

Imani's lips curled into a sensual smile as she traced her finger along the seam of his t-shirt. "I...don't know why I'm here, to be honest. Maybe I wanted to get to know you better. The real you, not the role model at the center, or the man that you present to the world because you're trying to protect yourself and not lose everything again. But I am here," she said, her tone dropping lower until it was almost a whisper, "so I am going to enjoy being here with you."

Desmond was still for a few beats, long enough for Imani to rethink what she'd just said and be prepared for him to ask her to leave. As it was, she wasn't exactly breaking any rules about fraternizing with the director of her pro bono project, but it was certainly inappropriate to be two shots in and curled up on his couch, close enough to sniff the scent of his cologne.

"I've got a sweet tooth," he admitted finally. "How about some wine and a little dessert?"

A few minutes later, they settled on the couch with their wine and a plate of cookies. Desmond picked a romantic movie to watch and turned the lamp down, dimming the room. The electricity that had been simmering between them from the moment they'd first made eye contact at Bright Pathways hummed in the air like a live wire.

As the sun set and the sky outside turned an inky purple-black, they sat together on the couch, thighs touching, indulging in wine and each other's company. Imani felt relaxed and more at ease than she had in years—even with Julian, which was strange to her. She shifted her position slightly, angling herself toward Desmond.

His eyes met hers, both drowning in the other's gaze. Imani's heart thundered in her chest as she reached out, her hand cupping his cheek as he looked at her, surprise and desire warring in his eyes.

She leaned in, pressing her lips to his in a tentative kiss.

Desmond responded immediately, his lips moving against hers, his fingers curling in her hair as he deepened the kiss. Imani moaned into his mouth, eliciting a moan from him in return.

He slid his arms around her, pulling her closer while their tongues danced in a passionate tango. His grip on her hips tightened, anchoring her to him as if he was afraid she might slip away if he let go.

Imani's hands roamed his chest, crossed his shoulders, traveled the contours of his muscles through his t-shirt. She wasn't sure if it was the wine or Desmond, but she almost couldn't bear the heat between them.

"God, I'm hot," she moaned, tearing her lips from his.

Without words, Desmond began to pull her t-shirt up. She raised her arms to let him remove it. Tossing it to the couch behind her, he took in the sight of her like she was something he'd been longing for.

Desmond's hands roamed Imani's bare skin, leaving a trail of goosebumps in their wake. She leaned into his touch, reveling in the sensation. She was on fire, every nerve ending tingling.

His lips trailed the line of her neck, nipping and kissing until he reached the lace cup of her bra. He looked up at her as if to ask for permission. She gripped the back of his head and pulled him in, her breath hitching when his teeth closed around her nipple through the fabric.

The moans that rolled from her mouth as he sucked and nipped at her breasts sent shivers down her spine. She was here, mentally begging this man she barely knew to never

ever stop pleasing her this way...but when she looked into his hooded eyes, all her reservations melted away.

"God, I love that," she mumbled. He chuckled low in his throat, sending vibrations shooting straight to her core.

"Yeah? You want more?"

"Yes, yes, yes. So much more."

Desmond paused and looked up at her, his gaze filled with heat and need, but also the slightest hesitation. "You know what you're doing, Imani? What you're walking into?"

She moved her hands down to the waistband of his jeans, fumbling with the button and zipper. Desmond let out a low groan as she wrapped her warm hand around him. His hips bucked involuntarily into her touch and he had to force himself to chill before it was over too soon.

"I guess that's a yes," Desmond said. "But...not here."

He stood, pulling Imani with him to the end of the room where his bed was made with crisp white sheets and a slate grey down comforter. The headboard had a pile of pillows against it and a nightstand held another lamp and a stack of books.

Imani crawled onto the bed, shedding her clothing before getting comfortable.

"Who said you got the middle?" Desmond joked, pulling open a drawer in the nightstand and digging for something under a pile of envelopes and other objects.

"Looks like you keep condoms in a junk drawer, so I'm not sure you deserve to be in the middle of the bed."

"This ain't no junk drawer," he said, pulling out a box and tearing off the plastic film. "This is where I keep important shit. Birth certificate, freedom papers, condoms."

"Freedom papers," she repeated.

"Yeah. You want to read them before we get down? Make sure I'm telling you the truth?"

Imani laughed. "You know I googled you as soon as I got home. Stop playing and suit up."

"I did assume that. And I was playin'."

He pulled a condom from the box and rolled it on, then crawled onto the bed with her. "Now, was I right here?" he purred, nibbling on her earlobe.

"Nuh-uh. You were lower and heading further south."

"My bad. Let me catch up."

His lips trailed hot, wet kisses around her collarbone, moving lower until he reached her breasts again. He teased her nipples until they were both hard pebbles, then he kissed down her belly, his fingertips dancing over her hips and finding their way between her thighs.

She moaned, bending to his touch. Desmond didn't hesitate to dive in, his tongue lapping at her clit and sending sparks coursing through her. Imani's grip on the comforter tightened as he drove her higher and higher.

"Oh...oh, shit! Desmond! Yes!"

Desmond's tongue and fingers were sinfully skilled, sending her spiraling toward the kind of orgasm she'd been starved for. She writhed beneath him as if he orchestrated her movements from his place between her legs until she was on the edge, her body trembling, her moans growing louder.

"I'm gonna fucking come!" she squealed.

"You better," he paused long enough to say before he inserted two fingers inside her while flicking his tongue against her clit so light, the sensation was like butterfly wings.

"Fuck!" she screeched. Imani's mind was a blur—she needed more pressure, more friction. She laid her hands on his head and pressed his face into her, rolling her clit against his tongue until pulses of pleasure coursed through her like an endless tsunami of orgasmic waves.

Her climax left her boneless and spent and involuntarily shuddering. Her arms were splayed at her sides and her legs would likely not hold her up if she tried to stand.

Desmond crawled up the bed, positioning himself above her. "You ready for me?" he asked, his voice husky. "Or do you need a minute?"

"Oh, don't you dare make me wait," she breathed, laughing while gripping his hips and pulling him close. "Gimme. And don't be shy about it."

Desmond positioned himself and, without another word, entered her. In a few swift thrusts, she was deliriously full of him. Imani gasped as his length stretched her walls in a way that made her head spin. She locked her limbs around him, pulling him closer as they moved together.

"Mmmm... *fuck*," she moaned, the pleasure building with every thrust. He filled her so perfectly, hitting every good spot, leaving nothing untouched.

This, this, this, this! *This* was what she needed. What she was craving. Scratching an itch had never felt so delicious.

"God *damn*," Desmond groaned into her ear as he sped up his pace, each thrust more powerful than the last. "This pussy is so...*fuckin'* good. Shit!"

Imani clung to him, lost in the sensations coursing through her. Desmond was relentless, his thrusts now more urgent as they both chased release. The sound of their bodies slapping together echoed in the room, drowned out by moans and gasps and guttural grunts.

"My God, Imani," Desmond groaned as he buried his

face in the crook of her neck. "You feel amazing. I never want to stop."

Imani mumbled something she hoped Desmond took as encouragement. She could barely form a coherent thought. Every touch, every thrust drove her higher until she was completely adrift, lost in the moment, in him.

Desmond's hand slid between them, his fingers finding her clit and stroking circles that set the spiral winding through her core.

"I want you to come with me, Desmond," she whimpered.

"Go ahead. I'm right behind you, girl." Desmond grunted, his hips moving faster, thrusting hard.

The orgasm hit her in a rush, her entire body tensing as her climax rocked through her. "I'm coming, I'm coming! I'm fucking coming..."

Desmond's thrusts became more frenzied as he felt Imani's walls clench around him, triggering his own release. "Fuck, fuck, fuck, fuck!"

He let out a deep, low groan as he emptied himself inside of her, their bodies trembling and shaking together. Desmond lost most of his strength and collapsed on top of her, still inside her, both trying to catch their breath.

"That was..." Imani trailed off. "I have no words."

"I could think of a few, but I need a minute."

Desmond's lips found hers again as they came down together, clinging to each other like life rafts. He rolled off her onto his side. She scooted close to him, up against his chest as he wrapped an arm around her.

Imani's breathing returned to normal first, and she propped herself up on her elbow. She found Desmond's eyes, a shy smile playing on her lips.

"Was that supposed to happen?" Desmond whispered.

"I'm thinking no," she answered. "I have no regrets."

"Good. Because I don't, either. Are you in a hurry to leave?"

"Are you asking me what I'm about to do?"

A gut-level bark of laughter rolled from Desmond. "Naw, girl. I was going to get us some water and a snack and suggest you get up under the covers before you get cold."

"You know what I'm kind of in the mood for?"

"More of what I just gave you?"

"I mean...yes. But you should make this ramen you're always bragging about."

"I think you're trying to take me down a peg by talking about my ramen after I gave you a good— what did you call it? Hot...sixteen—"

"Sixteen pumps!" Imani finished, uncontrollably giggling. "If you feel like your ramen isn't up to the job, the water is fine."

"See, what you're not going to do is insult my prison ramen. Get ready for a culinary delight as soon as I get rid of this condom."

After using the bathroom to freshen up, Imani picked up Desmond's t-shirt from the couch and pulled it on, then slid between the cool sheets and pulled the comforter up to her chin. She watched him move about the kitchenette with ease and skill.

Admired the way her thighs were sore and her throat was dry and her lips plump from being ravished.

Also ignored the tiny blinking red warning light flashing inside her head.

She was in trouble.

TEN

DESMOND

SUNLIGHT CREPT THROUGH THE CURTAINS, casting a glow across Desmond's small, cozy studio. He stirred, his dream slipping away as he blinked awake. The memory of his weekend with Imani lingered between sleep and consciousness. It had replayed in his head since she got in her car Sunday afternoon to go home.

Desmond reached for his phone and squinted at the screen. 4:58 AM. Really? Two minutes ahead of the alarm? He opened the texting app and re-read Imani's message from the night before.

> I'm going to be walking into the office like I was horseback riding all weekend. Thanks for that.

A smile tugged at the corner of his mouth as he turned off the alarm and scrolled to a daily news podcast, then flipped the covers back. The routine of his morning—make the bed, work out, have breakfast, shower, a quick check on Beyond Bars, then head to work—felt lighter, more purposeful.

Or maybe he was just a happy man because he got his dick wet, as the kids say. He hoped he would have a chance to do more of that soon.

A few hours passed before he emerged from his apartment, dressed for the day with a satchel slung over his shoulder. The weekday rush surrounded him. He waved at children waiting for their school bus and nodded to drivers speeding past. Living a few blocks from Bright Pathways made the brisk walk worthwhile most mornings.

Twenty minutes later, he walked through the double doors. He gave his usual nod to Marcelle, who sat behind the tall half-circle reception desk that concealed a multi-line phone and an ancient computer connected to an ink-hungry printer. She pushed her glasses down her nose and fixed him with a pointed stare.

"Just who I was lookin' for. Mornin', Desmond," she said, her fingers drumming against the desk. "I hope you've had your Wheaties today."

He slowed his pace. "Had my Wheaties? Now, that's something my grandmama would say. What's going on?"

"Caleb's waiting for you in the lounge." Her brows lifted as she nodded toward the hallway. "I tried to run him off, but he said he wanted to wait for you. Got his lips all twisted up like somethin' worrisome is on his mind."

Desmond frowned. Caleb should be heading to school. Though he could write excuse notes for foster kids in his care, he used that power sparingly. Whatever brought Caleb here this early needed attention. "I'll go see what's up."

A tense-looking Caleb sat on one of the worn couches, his hands clasped between his knees. "Sup, Desmond?"

"You tell me," Desmond said. He closed the door, pulled a chair near the couch, and lowered himself to meet Caleb's eyes. "Marcelle said you had something on your mind."

"Did you mean that stuff you said about how this is a safe space and we can come to you to talk about anything?"

"Absolutely," he answered. "Talk to me."

Caleb looked up. His eyes were watery, swollen and red-rimmed. "Me and Caesar...well, we partied over the weekend. I had a curfew and I didn't want to get in trouble, so I left. Caesar's foster parents don't really keep tabs on him these days. He said he was going to stay. After I left, somebody called the cops on the noise, I guess. He got swept up, and he's still in jail. His foster mom might get him and she might not. I'm worried about him, though. He talks tough, but he don't know shit about jail."

Cold recognition washed through Desmond as memories of his first days in custody threatened to surface. He exhaled, dragging a hand across his forehead, but stopped when he caught Caleb's stricken expression. The boy was right to worry. Desmond knew how quickly the system could swallow a kid like Caesar whole and set him on a path hard to escape.

"Okay. I have his foster mom's number—I'll start there and see what's up. Maybe I'll go down to the jail with her. Thanks for letting me know about this. You need to get to school before you get into trouble too. I can't help Caesar if I'm helping you."

Caleb nodded but hesitated. "I heard you know a lot about jail. Prison, actually. Is he gonna be okay? Is there anything you can do to help him?"

The words hit Desmond like a punch to the gut. He had

never shared his past with any of the kids. As far as he was concerned, it was private information that none of them needed to know.

"Where did you hear that I know about prison?"

Caleb shrugged. "We are, as they say, extremely online. It don't take but ten seconds to read everything about you."

Tension crept into Desmond's shoulders as he let out a long breath. He'd forgotten how connected kids were these days.

"It's, uhm... It's not something I like talking about. I wouldn't want anyone to take it as bragging or gloating. It's nothing to aspire to. But yeah, it can be fucked up in there. I'll do everything I can to help him, alright?"

"Yeah." Relief softened Caleb's features as he stood and adjusted his full backpack. "You mind giving me an update when you see him?"

"I'll do that. You do the same." Desmond held out his hand. Caleb grabbed it to shake, then caught Desmond off guard when he pulled him close and wrapped his other arm around his torso.

"Thanks, Mr. Taylor."

"Man, get out of here with that Mr. Taylor stuff."

Alone in the lounge, Desmond filled his lungs with air and released it slowly, trying to calm the anxiety rolling through him. The start of the week had shown such promise —waking up next to Imani, her warm body pressed against his erection and a breast in his palm. Even after she left his apartment, the day went well. He'd had a great session with his group on Beyond Bars and caught up on his daily reading.

Then Monday had dawned and...this was how it was going to go?

Desmond knew how quickly the system could derail a

life, how easy it was to slip between the cracks. He couldn't let that happen to Caesar. At his desk, he pulled open a drawer and rifled through his files to locate Caesar's information sheet.

DESMOND ARRIVED at Fulton County Jail alongside Geena, Caesar's foster mother. Her steps seemed quick and determined, as if the faster she walked, the sooner she could deal with Caesar's case and leave. Her dark sunglasses hid her eyes but could not conceal the tight set of her lips, slathered in a glossy pink. It was clear she was not in a good mood, but she had agreed to this meeting with Desmond and their lawyer.

The sharp scent of bleach and the tang of body odor filled his nose as they walked past stone-faced officers. Their footsteps bounced off bare walls in the stark hallways. Every detail brought back memories he'd rather forget.

They were eventually led to a small room where Caesar was waiting with the family attorney, a stocky man in a suit with salt and pepper hair and thick glasses. Caesar looked like a lost puppy in a misshapen dark blue short-sleeved shirt and pants. His usual swag was replaced by a pensive, nervous expression. He stood when they entered the room, his face lighting up at the sight of Desmond and Geena. Despite her anger, she let Caesar hug her, wrapping his arms around her slight shoulders.

"I'm sorry!" he began. "I didn't mean to get picked up. I was just hanging out when the cops showed up."

"Alright, alright," she said, pulling away and taking a seat. "I don't have time for this mess. I've got to get back to the kids. You tell your lawyer what happened?"

Caesar sat. "Yeah. On God, no cap, I was on the porch, hanging with some dudes talking when a bunch of cops pulled up. I froze. Didn't move or nothin'. I didn't have anything on me, I hadn't even been drinking. I was literally just there. They grabbed me with everybody else, said just shut up and come on. They haven't even charged me yet. Right?"

He glanced at the attorney, who shrugged. "It's early yet. I can't promise there won't be charges. He's being held, probably so they can dig up something to stick him with."

Desmond nodded, understanding this game all too well. "What are the chances you can talk to the arresting officer? He's a minor, he has no record. I've been working with him at Bright Pathways and I'm willing to vouch for him."

The attorney hesitated, then frowned. "I'll need to check out the arrest report, make sure they don't have anything on him. If it all checks out, I'll petition for a release into his foster mother's custody. But if you vouch for him, you've got to help him stay out of trouble—the next stop is considerable jail time or a boot camp. He won't get a second chance."

"If you get me outta here, I won't let you down," Caesar said. "I just want to get home. This shit ain't for me. I'm so serious, I ain't coming back here."

Desmond glanced at Geena, then back at the boy. "Getting you out is up to your lawyer, but come see me when you're released, Caesar. We'll work on a plan to keep you too busy to get in trouble. Understand?"

"Yes, sir."

Desmond left the jail, leaving Geena and her lawyer to work out the details of Caesar's release.

Each step away from the jail lifted a weight, but the memories clung to him. The sound of iron doors closing, voices echoing off concrete, the loss of freedom—it all felt too fresh. Years had passed since his confinement, but the urge to escape back to his life of choice and movement pulled at him.

Caesar's arrest painted a stark picture of consequences. Desmond refused to watch history repeat itself. The kids at the center deserved better chances than he'd had. They deserved real shots at bright futures.

Desmond returned to Bright Pathways and parked his car in the front lot. Denise looked up from the *Atlanta Journal-Constitution* pages at her desk.

"I thought that was you. I didn't even know you drove."

"I live close. No sense in wasting the gas every day, but today I had to go downtown. I'm way behind, so I'll be at my desk until the after-school crowd arrives."

"How is Caesar doing? You get to see him?" Desmond's head tilted in surprise before he could hide it. "You know Marcelle is a gossip. She said Caleb was in here early this morning to talk to you about Caesar getting arrested over the weekend. Is he alright?"

"I saw him. He seemed fine, considering."

Denise hummed, her lips pursed. "He getting out or are they holding him?"

"I don't know yet. I should have an update in a few hours. Keep your fingers crossed that they let him go."

"I'll get my prayer team on it. Hold up, though..." She waved a page of the newspaper in front of him. "You see this article in the paper about the governor proposing a cut to social programs in next year's budget?"

That was the last thing he wanted or expected to see. "No, I haven't had the chance to look at the paper today. What does it say?"

Denise handed him the page, poking the byline with

her finger. "It says here that the governor is proposing a slimmer budget next year. A grip of programs are on the chopping block, including grants for social programs. Aren't we one of those social programs?"

His stomach twisted into knots as he carefully read through the article. "The majority of our operating expenses are paid out of a grant from the state, yeah. I guess I need to figure out which programs he's cutting."

Loss of state funding would gut the before- and after-school programs, summer camps, mentorships, field trips, and other extracurricular activities that were so important for childhood development. They would have to cut back on staff and resources, making it harder to provide quality care and support for the children that came through their doors.

Beyond that, his livelihood hung in the balance. This center wasn't just a job—it was his purpose. The thought of it closing when students like Caleb and Caesar depended on it made his chest tight.

"I'll check this out," he said. "Thanks for bringing it to my attention."

He headed down the hall to the lounge, closing the door behind him. At his desk, he pulled up the newspaper website and found the article, searching through the referenced links. He read it thoroughly, his heart sinking with each word. Bright Pathways was already operating on a shoestring budget. This could be devastating.

Desmond leaned back in his chair, pressing his fingers against his temples as he processed the implications. The article called it a proposal, not a done deal. Even if it passed, the center had funding through next year's grant deadline.

There's time, he thought, soothing himself. *There's time to research options.*

He pulled out his phone, scrolling through his contacts until he found Imani's number. His thumb hovered over the call button. She worked for a financial firm that helped businesses manage their money. Maybe she'd have insight or connections that could help.

But he couldn't make himself press the button to connect the call. She did say she was available for him as well as the attendees, but it was too soon to involve her in his life's problems. He didn't want to come across as needy or opportunistic; that wasn't what she signed up for.

He pressed the button to lock the phone, then dropped it into a pocket in his backpack and shoved the bag into a drawer. He had plenty of work to catch up on before the room filled with loud, sweaty teenagers. While he still could, there were bills to pay, schedules to finish and publish, and reports to complete. Desmond dove into his work, trying to push the worries about funding to the back of his mind.

The day raced past in a blur of perpetual catch-up. Just as exhaustion settled in, Caleb burst into the room grinning, bouncing on his toes. He'd heard from Caesar—released without charges and finally home.

"The DA decided not to charge him since the officers didn't find anything on him and they never did a field sobriety test. He'll be at school tomorrow and he'll be down here after that."

Desmond offered a celebratory fist bump. "I told his foster mom that we'd be working on a deal aimed at improving his behavior. You might want to plan on hanging out at Caesar's house for the foreseeable future. He's about to have a lot of free time—no hanging out, no partying, no going out. He's on their radar now, and you by association. You feel me?"

"Felt," Caleb said, his smile fading slightly. "Caesar was shook."

"I can relate," Desmond acknowledged with a nod. "How about you round up some fellas for a game of hoops out back before we lose daylight?"

After the last child had been picked up and the center was quiet, Desmond locked himself in the lounge. His eyes burned as he stared at the computer screen, scrolling through endless lists of grants and funding opportunities. He'd been at it for hours, long after the janitor had come through and gone.

The quiet of the empty center gave him time and space to process the day's events. Caesar's close call, the looming budget cuts, his own unresolved past. So much seemed out of his control. He wouldn't be able to keep Caesar safe, no matter how hard he tried. Most of the grants he found to help fund Bright Pathways were either too small to make a real difference or had such specific requirements that the center didn't qualify.

Desmond rubbed his eyes, the weight of responsibility heavy on his shoulders. His phone buzzed, startling him. A text from Imani lit up the screen:

Hey. You around?

He smiled, her words providing a brief respite. His thumbs hovered over the keyboard as he debated how to respond. Her warmth and understanding felt like a lifeline he desperately needed, but she had no idea what she was getting herself into. He was of the mind to slowly integrate her into his life and give her every opportunity to bow out if needed.

Still at work actually,

he ended up typing.

Roller coasters are jealous of how up and down this day has been.

Sounds rough. Need to talk?

Desmond hesitated, again tempted to unload. Again, he resisted.

I would like nothing better than to dump all my problems on you. Preferably while next to you in bed after I wear you out.

That sounds like the best idea ever, honestly. I sense a but coming...

But...

He chuckled, pausing for dramatics.

I've got some things happening around here that really deserve my attention. I'm not ready to download yet.

The offer stands when you're ready. So... you don't want to talk at all? I could keep you company on the walk home.

I actually drove today. That's how wild the day has been.

Wow. You never drive. I can't wait to hear what happened.

Desmond smiled, touched by Imani's concern.

> It's a long story. I promise to fill you in soon.

> Don't work too late. Even superheroes need rest.

> Thanks. I'm wrapping up soon.

Desmond paused, then added,

> Don't get it twisted, you've been on my mind. It kinda hurt to not have you hogging the bed last night.

> I wasn't hogging shit, the way you plastered yourself up against me. There was plenty of bed available.

Desmond chuckled.

> You're right about that. I needed to soak up all that soft skin.

> Not gonna lie... I ran a few scenes back in my mind.

> I can imagine which ones.

For a moment, he let himself get lost in flashes of their weekend together—her supple skin under his fingertips, the taste of her lips, the feel of her body pressed into him, the seduction in her voice as she moaned in chorus with him. His body was responding, ready to go down that path.

> I am happy to hear that I've been on your mind. I was hoping you weren't trying to be a one-night stand.

> Absolutely the fuck not

He wrote back.

> Good to hear because the way I'm craving you…

> I put it down, is what you're saying? Gave you a hot sixteen pumps?

> …a few times.

Desmond felt a rush of heat course through him, and he shifted in his chair as he fought his body's reaction to her words.

> Careful now. I'm about to be in a compromising position.

> Oh? Which position might that be?

> I'm sure you'd like to know…

> I would, actually. In specific, sexy detail.

He laughed, shaking his head.

> You're trouble, woman. I gotta finish up here, but… maybe I'll call you once I'm in the bed.

> Oh, please do. Tell me a bedtime story.

> Bet. I need to get back to work before you derail me any more.

> Alright, alright. Go be responsible. But don't keep me waiting.

Desmond closed the messaging app and placed his phone on the table, savoring their playful exchange. It had been ages since he had flirted like that. But as he looked back at his computer screen, reality crashed back in. The list of potential grants and tasks seemed endless.

He pushed through his remaining work. Over an hour later, he shut down his computer and headed to his truck.

At home, he showered and changed, warmed up leftovers, and ate while checking Beyond Bars. After dinner, he washed his dishes, brushed his teeth, applied moisturizer, and pulled back the covers.

Settled in bed, Desmond grabbed his phone and scrolled to Imani's name. Excitement fluttered in his belly as he pressed call. After one ring, her sultry voice filled his ears.

"I thought you'd never call," she purred, sending a shiver down his spine.

"You thought wrong," Desmond replied, sinking deeper into the cool sheets.

ELEVEN

IMANI

IMANI SIGHED as she ended the call with Desmond. Their playful banter had been a reprieve from the monotony of her day, but now, alone in her quiet bedroom, her thoughts were a jumble.

Three days ago, his photo appeared on her Instagram's 'people you may know' banner. She'd spent twenty minutes scrolling through his sparse feed—scenic photos, shots of Bright Pathways during renovation, and his freshly washed pickup truck. Something about his confident smile in those pictures made her pause. Instead of scrolling past, she'd taken a chance.

Already, she couldn't stop thinking about him. There was an undeniable connection—physically, emotionally, intellectually. Imani hadn't felt this way about someone in a very long time, which...could be dangerous.

The ghost of Julian's memory crept in. Was she ready to dive into something meaningful? To toss her still-mending heart back into the fray? Could she risk getting involved with Desmond, even if it could jeopardize her position at work?

Not that it mattered because she'd been disconnected from her projects for some time.

With a groan, she flopped back onto a plush pile of pillows and a thick duvet. The internal conflict was giving her a headache. She wished she could talk it through with Casey, but she had been away on an anniversary trip with her husband and wouldn't return until later that evening. Besides, Imani didn't want to interrupt her celebration of thirty years of wedded bliss to talk through her crush on an ex-convict.

Logic told her to guard her heart. Move slowly, be careful and cautious. But that was boring. She wanted to take the decidedly more fun but dangerous path—throw caution to the wind and explore the magnetic pull between her and Desmond. Surely she deserved to have some fun after what Julian put her through.

Her phone lit up with a text from Desmond:

> Have the most beautiful sleep. Hoping I dream about you.

Imani smiled, feeling a flush spread through her. She quickly typed back:

> You'll be starring in my dreams tonight too. Excited to do more than dream about each other soon.

Setting her phone aside, she got up to begin her bedtime routine, applying moisturizer to her face and a whitening strip to her teeth. As she stood in front of the mirror rubbing lotion into her skin, her mind wandered back into dangerous territory.

What if...she showed up to Desmond's place unannounced wearing nothing but a thin, silky negligee?

What if...without warning, he pulled her into his studio and slammed the door shut behind them, and then, with fire in his eyes, pushed her up against the wall and pressed his body against hers? She could almost feel his breath on her neck as he leaned in, his grip tightening on her waist.

What if... she surrendered to those primal, carnal urges and shamelessly ground herself against that throbbing, meaty bulge that fit so perfectly between her thighs?

What if...his lips traveled a path along the peaks and valleys of her body until he ended up on his knees with one of her legs draped over his shoulder while his tongue alternated between bathing her clit and slipping into her slick entrance?

Imani shuddered at the scene playing out in her imagination: Desmond teasing her, taking his time to build up anticipation before finally standing and unfurling himself. She widened her stance as she imagined him parting her legs, then sliding inside her, filling her in a single stroke. His body pressed against hers, her hips rolling in response to his perfect rhythm.

Imani gasped aloud, barely registering one hand twisting a taut nipple, the other mimicking his thrusts.

"Desmond," she whimpered aloud, her voice bouncing against the tile in her bathroom.

Her body undulated in arousal as she imagined digging her nails into the dark skin across his broad shoulders, pushing out the most delicious sounds as he pinned her against the door and thrust into her with an intensity that left her breathless. She let her mind wander further, bringing her an exquisite pleasure as she dreamed of their bodies moving together in harmony, their hips meeting in a primal rhythm.

"*Yesss,*" she hissed, imagining Desmond growling her name as he lost himself in the moment.

The images were so vivid, the sensation so real, Imani could almost smell his cologne mingling with the scents of sex in the air.

"Fuck me!" she whispered, then bit her lip in an attempt to stifle the cries that wanted to spill from her mouth. Control slipped away and she let loose with sexy, throaty commands that she only hoped would bring Desmond to climax with her. "Harder! God, yes! Shit! Desmond! Oh God, yes! Yes! *YES!*"

Imani's eyes snapped open. She didn't recognize herself in the mirror, one hand clutching a breast, the other between her thighs as she rode the crest of a convulsive orgasm fueled by a horny fantasy of Desmond doing nasty things to her.

Heat consumed her as the pulsing vibrations faded. Her breaths came in ragged gasps and her chest heaved as she struggled to catch her breath. Beads of sweat coated her brow, and the room was warm...so warm.

Desmond had wormed his way into her fantasies, and she was helpless to do anything about it.

Still shaking, Imani turned on the shower and removed the whitening strip. When she had completed her evening routine, she went back to her bedroom and pulled the duvet back, moved a few pillows to the chair next to her bed, and slid between the sheets, cool and silky against her over-heated skin.

She picked up her phone again to the messaging app. Desmond had replied to her last text.

> Excited about that too, Imani. See you Thursday.

In response, she typed,

> Can't. Wait.

Then she hit send before she could overthink it, set her phone on the nightstand charger, and rolled onto her side, hoping her racing imagination would let her rest.

HER ALARM JERKED her from vivid dreams the next morning. She fumbled to silence it, rubbing sleep from her eyes. As she pulled the scarf from her two-strand twists, her phone lit up with a new message.

> Hope you slept well because you kept me up half the night.

She bit her lip to suppress a grin and quickly typed back,

> Could say the same about you.

By the time Imani arrived at the office, she was thoroughly distracted and not at all looking forward to her workday. The only comfort was that there was only one more day until she would see Desmond.

As she mechanically booted up her computer, reviewed her schedule, and responded to emails, her mind was elsewhere. The financial statements in front of her were a blur of numbers as she fixated on thoughts of broad shoulders, full lips, and strong hands that could make her pulse race.

Imani took her lunch at her desk with her office door closed. Casey had returned from vacation late the evening before, and since they hadn't spoken since happy hour the week prior, there was so much news to share.

"Hey girl, hey," she answered when the FaceTime notification came through. Casey was at her desk in her home office, her skin glowing with a golden tan. "I know you're just back from sunny beaches and daily massages, but your girl needs a quick check-in."

"I am just barely off the plane from Jamaica and we already have to talk about Desmond?"

"We don't have to talk about Desmond at all, actually..."

"I texted you Saturday night and your sneaky behind didn't answer until Sunday afternoon. You are never busy these days. So it would seem we do indeed need to talk about Desmond."

Imani laughed as she lightly tossed vinaigrette dressing through a salad. "I don't even know where to start."

"You got yourself all twisted up again?"

"No, not really. Well..." She bounced her head side to side. "Maybe a little twisted. But it's more internal than anything else."

"Internal like you know you need to leave him alone but the coochie be callin' out to him?"

Imani sighed. "When you put it that way..."

"Wasn't finding out your previous lover was married after he died enough excitement for you? I would think you'd love a little boredom right now."

"You would think," Imani said before shoving a large forkful of salad into her mouth.

"Since you're determined to make life exciting for yourself, how are things with Mr. Tall, Dark, and Felonious?"

Imani snorted, almost choking on her lunch. "Still tall, still dark. Not a felon, though, remember? He was cleared, nothing on his record."

"Right. Yeah, I did find that out."

Casey's job as an Assessment Specialist meant she had access to programs to research security clearances. Using that kind of power for personal gain was frowned upon and Imani never wanted Casey to risk her job to keep her out of trouble. Not to be deterred, Casey had used a regular web browser and consumer programs to investigate Desmond's claims that he'd been wrongly accused, then released, and his criminal record had been expunged.

"I don't know what to do," Imani whined. "I know what common sense says. I know I'm too old to be falling so hard for some man I barely know—"

"But you also know that you're not going to be happy if you don't at least give things a good chance. And you're right about that. So just go for it."

"Uh...hello?" Imani tapped the phone screen. "Am I speaking to an alien pod? Please put Casey back on the line because she would never advise me to actually follow my heart."

"Liar. I would so advise you to do that. You overthink everything, Imani. It's just like with Julian. There was nothing wrong with getting your cheeks clapped once a fortnight. Nobody told you to be thinking about relocating to North Carolina to be with him. Have some fun, let loose. But don't jump off the deep end. Don't call me next month talking about how you and Desmond are about to buy some old shack of a house in southwest Atlanta. You hear me, girl?"

Imani rolled her eyes as she threw the last dregs of her salad in the trash. "I will not be buying some old shack of a house in southwest Atlanta with Desmond." After a pause, she giggled and added, "There are some cute new town-homes going up out there. We'd get one of those."

Casey groaned. "Maybe you just need a little somethin' to get your groove back. Just know that's all it is."

Imani chewed her lip. "I don't know...it could be more than that."

"But you don't know that right now. A few orgasms won't hurt a damn thing, but they don't mean shit either. Leave your heart out of it." Casey chuckled. "And your mind, too. That bitch don't know what she's doing. Leave things to your Nice One. She's the only one empowered to make the decisions right now."

"Casey. You did not just refer to my lady parts as Nice One."

Casey's laugh rumbled from the depths of her chest. "That's what my mama used to call it in our girl talks. I'm sure Desmond agrees she is quite nice."

"And does. Mr. Joyner must have dicked you down on vacation. Came home wanting everybody feeling good, huh?"

"He did not neglect me, I'll tell you that much. I'm just glad to see you laughing again. If Desmond makes you smile, and he makes you feel wanted, and he isn't married or wanted by the police, I'm here for it. Just be safe, okay? Go on and wax all of the things and whatever else y'all are into nowadays."

They chatted until work called Imani back, but her mind was already on Thursday.

IMANI TOOK extra care getting ready for work, choosing a wrap dress that clung to every curve and heels that made her legs look amazing. She left her hair down, letting the twists hang around her shoulders.

The workday had dragged by in slow motion, every second crawling until she could leave the building and head south. As she walked down the hallway to the community center lounge, she was nervous that Desmond was mere steps away. She forced herself to slow down.

Don't rush, don't make it obvious.

The room was loud and full of young people racing around, exerting pent-up energy. Desmond was at his desk, leaning back in his chair with muscled arms folded across his chest, in a relaxed pose while surrounded by a group of boys. As if he sensed she had entered the room, he turned his head toward her. They locked eyes for a few seconds before Desmond returned his attention to the boys around him. After a quiet word, they dispersed and settled into the chairs and couches in the center of the room.

He rose from his desk and approached her, his eyes traveling the length of her body. "Imani, it's good to see you," he said, attempting to lower his voice and maintain a professional tone but failing at both.

Imani nodded, fighting her body's reaction to being in his vicinity. "Thank you. Great seeing you as well."

His eyes darkened and she tore her gaze from his, turning to greet a few of the kids. Desmond cleared his throat, moving back to the desk.

"That's my cue to start us off."

He reached for the remote and pointed it at the TV, silencing it and getting everyone's attention.

"Okay, everyone. Let's get started. It's our second-to-last

session with Ms. Imani. Who did the homework from last week and wants to share what they found?"

The next hour and a half passed in a blink as the group had a lively session discussing banks, credit unions, savings accounts, and financial tips for young adults. Imani was impressed with how involved each of them were in the discussion. She loved the real-life, real-world questions that arose. She felt needed and useful, and somehow, though she had been dreading the assignment, these evenings at Bright Pathways had become her favorite few hours of the week.

"Are we not gonna talk about what happened this weekend with Caesar?" Deja asked after the workshop had ended and the group was packing up. "We're in this group to talk about real-life stuff and we're just going to let it fly by?"

Imani glanced at Desmond, who sought out Caesar in the group. He'd been quiet, uncharacteristically so. Caesar was usually good for an inappropriate quip, but aside from a few questions, he seemed like a different young man tonight.

"It would be up to Caesar to talk about his weekend," Desmond said. "I wasn't going to violate his privacy, so yes, I had planned to table that discussion for another time."

The teens collectively groaned. "Man," grumbled Chloe from the back of the room. "I was looking forward to the real recap, not the PC version I've been hearing."

"I don't mind talking about it," Caesar said, surprising everyone. He stood, pulling the long sleeves of his sweat-shirt down, and stepped to the front of the room. "If you don't mind me taking over the session, Ms. Imani, I might could use some of that good advice you be having."

Imani stepped aside, giving Caesar the floor and taking a seat next to Desmond.

"So, last weekend," he began, "I partied a little too hard. I've been running with this crew, some older guys involved in a lot of different stuff. I wasn't involved in any of that, I just wanted to be cool. I was out on the porch at this house party when a bunch of cops pulled up. Lights and everything. They pop out of their cars and rush the house and just start grabbing people. I said I wasn't on anything, didn't have anything, I wasn't even drunk, so what was I being arrested for?"

While the kids listened, Imani glanced over at Desmond. His eyes were locked on Caesar, his face an impassive mask, but she could tell by the way his jaw clenched and unclenched that he was just as affected by the story as she was.

"The cops said some bull about me being in the wrong place at the wrong time and hauled my ass to the station. Locked me up with..." His voice trailed off. "Scariest night of my life for real. And since it was the weekend, I was in there until Monday when Desmond called my foster mom. They were probably trying to find something to charge me with, but they decided it wasn't worth it, I guess."

Caesar went on to explain that he'd been released without charges, but it had shaken him up enough to think about his life choices.

"I don't want to go through that again. I know some dudes think jail or prison is a badge of honor, but that life ain't for me. I was only in for a few days, but it seems like a hard life. I've been talking to my foster mom and I'm going to be meeting with Desmond about keeping out of trouble, staying off the radar, stuff like that. So...that's it."

He shrugged, then shoved his hands into his pockets.

Desmond stood, approaching Caesar, and dropped an arm across his shoulders.

"So, if Caesar is going to be brave, so am I. There's a part of my past that I don't talk about here, but a little birdie told me that a lot of you already know. It's time to share that experience with you all, and I hope you listen, take these words to heart, and that you aren't judgmental about where I've been because it brought me here to you."

A room of teenagers had never been so quiet. With his arm still around Caesar, Desmond shared his story of getting caught up in an embezzlement and wire fraud scheme, being arrested, going to prison, and serving time in a prison camp.

"I can't say I'm proud of where I've been," Desmond added after sharing his story. "I can say that I'm proud of the man I became because I had to go through that. I still have a lot to work through, but my chief job right now is being here for you, guiding you through young adulthood and life in general and making sure you don't make the same mistakes I did. So Caesar..."

Desmond paused to face the young man, who stood stoic and quiet with glassy eyes and flushed skin. "I'm sorry that I wasn't more upfront about my past. I felt like it would deter from my mission here when it really could have helped show you that life in prison isn't an easy life. Life after prison isn't all that easy, either. Re-entry is a bitch, finding a good job is hard, and gaining respect is a real challenge. I hope I haven't lost yours."

"Not at all, man," said Caesar. "To be honest, I've been hardheaded my whole life. I can't say I'd really listen. I gotta learn shit the wrong way, the long way, the hard way before it's real for me. But yo, I appreciate your honesty, and for real, man... I want all the advice you and Ms. Imani got to help me stay upright."

Imani swiped an errant tear that rolled down her cheek.

"We've got you, Caesar," she said, standing and giving him a hug. "I'll do whatever I can to help."

The rest of the room echoed Imani's sentiment, with everyone standing and offering words of encouragement and support to Caesar.

"I've kept you all way past time," said Imani. "Next week is our last session, so let's make it a free-for-all, okay? A little Ask Me Anything. Bring all of your questions and I promise that if I can't answer them, I'll do some research and come back."

"What? You're bringing your fashions back down here by choice?" Deja asked.

"I promise. So make the questions hard—then I have to come back." Imani winked at the group, then waved them off as they filed out of the room.

When the room was empty and it was just Desmond and Imani, she let out a shaky sigh. "So...that was what you were dealing with on Monday when I texted you?"

"Part of it," Desmond replied, his expression grim. "But yeah. Twenty-four hours with you, followed by having to rouse Caesar's foster mom out of her house to go pick up her son from jail. And that's a place I never want to be again."

"I can't imagine you would ever want to step foot back in there, so the fact that you did means so much. But you... didn't want to tell me about that?"

Desmond hesitated before answering, his eyes downcast. "Well...you know..."

"Well, I know...what? My friend Casey thinks I should let you be some exploration and fun and nothing serious. Some sex, a few orgasms, a good time and nothing more. Is that what you think too? Am I wasting my time here?"

"No, Imani. You're not wasting your time. But it's going to take me a while to trust someone again."

The raw vulnerability in his words both scared and aroused her. His hand reached out toward hers, as if pleading for her understanding.

"I don't have people in my life that I trust like I want to trust you," he continued, his voice becoming more urgent. He waved a hand between them. "This is new and fun and exciting and fast. I'm not a man that jumps into something head first. Feet first. Heart first. I feel like I'm submerged and it's kind of scary, but also really nice. I don't want you to feel like I'm stepping back or pushing you away. I just need time."

"I can give you time," Imani whispered, her breath fanning across his face. "But you know I'm here for you, right? Eventually, you have to let me in."

Desmond nodded once and pulled her close. "Part of me wants to run from this. The other part of me wants to ask you over to my place because I need you to be here for me in a very specific way."

"I would be very interested in the latter half of that sentence," Imani said, pulling back just far enough to grab the handle of her bag and lead Desmond from the lounge. "I could tell you about the dream I had last night."

"I'd like to hear it. And, uh...you can tell me how your friend Casey knows about me."

TWELVE

IMANI

IMANI AND DESMOND rode back to his studio with Marvin Gaye and Tammi Terrell's "You're All I Need" pouring from the speakers on the short drive. Imani swung into the same spot she'd used a few days before and turned the car off.

As soon as they were inside, Desmond pulled her into his arms and caught her lips in a deep, sensuous kiss as he backed her against the door. Imani melted against him, her desire consuming any semblance of restraint she had. His fingers worked their way under the tie of her dress and pulled, loosening the fabric enough to reveal a lacy bra and panty set.

"You are so *got-damn* fine."

Imani blushed and bit her lip to stifle a moan as his fingers skimmed up her thighs to the edge of her lace panties. "I dreamed about you doing this to me last night. Right here. Just like this."

"Oh yeah? Tell me what I'm about to do then, baby girl."

Imani pulled him to her and whispered a few words in his ear. A grin slowly spread across his lips...then he laid those lips on her skin and began a journey from the sensitive spot under her earlobe, across her shoulders, both breasts, and the expanse of her belly until he was on his knees. He nibbled her clit through her panties, making sure it was erect before he hooked his thumbs under the elastic.

"You're wet for me, aren't you?" he almost purred as he slid her panties down her legs.

"Mmhmm..." Imani bit her lip, trying to keep from moaning too loudly so close to the hallway.

He chuckled and dipped his head lower, nibbling on her inner thighs, sending goosebumps up and down her spine. Then he was there, teasing her into a state of mindless pleasure.

"Ohhh...*yesssss*..." Imani moaned loudly, her fingers gripping his head as he continued to worship her. She wound her hips, grinding against his tongue.

"Did I do it like this in your dream?" he asked without taking his lips from her core.

Imani no longer cared if the neighbors could hear. "Fuck yes! Just like that. Oh my God, don't stop!"

Desmond chuckled as if he knew he had her exactly where he wanted her. He continued his assault, teasing, pulling, licking, sucking until Imani's knees buckled.

"Des—I'm...I'm coming..." She panted, her head thrown back and toes curling.

Desmond didn't relent until she screamed his name, gyrating as wave after wave of orgasm washed over her. He didn't give her a chance to catch her breath before he lifted her up, carried her across the room to the bed, and gently laid her down.

Quickly, Desmond disposed of his clothing, letting out a groan when she wrapped a hand around him, stroking slowly.

"My turn, huh?"

"I've been craving you all day," Imani confessed in a sultry whisper. "All week, actually."

"Same," Desmond whispered back. "Let me take care of something real quick, then I'm all yours."

As he had done before, Desmond retrieved a condom and rolled it on. Imani wasted no time shedding her dress and bra, letting them fall to the floor in a pile. She scooted back on the bed, pulling him with her, then gracefully moved on top of him.

His large hands gripped her hips as she positioned herself above him and then sank down, enveloping him in her slick heat. Imani's breath hitched as she rocked, creating a slow, sensual rhythm that coaxed deep, pleasured moans from them both.

They fell into sync, moving together urgently as if trying to make up for lost time. Imani rode him hard, grinding her hips against his, her breath coming in short gasps and moans. She had missed this over the past week— the raw passion, the intense physical and emotional connection. No daydream could ever compare to the real thing.

She leaned down, changing the angle, and captured his full lips in another searing kiss. Desmond responded by meeting her movements with powerful thrusts from below, hitting just the right spot at her core.

Imani cried out, feeling the pressure of her climax starting to build. He wrapped both arms around her and flipped them so he was on top, never once breaking the connection. She clutched Desmond's shoulders, her nails digging into his skin as he took control, thrusting into her with a force that made her body quake uncontrollably.

"This pussy is so good, baby," he grunted between thrusts as the head of his dick hit that sweet spot over and over again. "So...damn...good."

Imani fluttered around him and knew she was close.

"You comin'?" Desmond asked.

That was all it took to send her tumbling over the edge. Her back arched and she called out his name, her vision going white as the climax crashed over her. Desmond followed right after, gripping her so tightly she knew there would be marks left behind. He let out a long grunt as their bodies vibrated together.

Desmond rolled off of Imani and pulled her close up against him. She trailed her fingers idly across his muscular chest as she listened to his breathing slowly return to normal.

"So..." Desmond said after a few quiet moments had passed. "Casey is...your best friend, I'm guessing?"

"Yes. My road dog, my bestie, my A-1 since...well, since we worked together at my first job out of college."

"Okay. So her opinion matters, then?"

Imani couldn't help but laugh. "Yes, it does. And to be clear, she approves of this activity. Casey is just very protective of me, especially after...well, Julian."

"Uh-oh. Another name I don't know." Desmond rolled onto his side, propping himself up on one elbow. "Who is Julian?"

Imani hesitated. She hadn't meant to bring up Julian again so soon. Or ever. But Desmond had opened up to her, so it was only fair she do the same.

"Remember when I told you about my friend that died? Julian was more than a friend. We dated for a while. Almost a year. It was hot and heavy and getting serious. He asked me to move to Raleigh to be with him."

"Okay. But you don't live in Raleigh, and you're in my bed, so...he was a punk, huh?"

"He just disappeared one day. Wasn't calling, couldn't reach him, no responses to any messages. So I called him at work, where they informed me that he had died."

"Oh, damn, Imani..." Desmond reached out to comfort her. "That's a shitty way to find out."

"Oh, don't feel sorry for me. That's not the end of the story. The gal I talked to at his job tells me that if I want information on the services, I should reach out to his *wife*. She's making all of the arrangements."

"Wife? Damn, Imani!"

"Exactly. I felt like a fucking idiot. And like a dumbass, I dragged Casey to the funeral. The wife comes out and yells at me, tells me I'm not welcome there. Like I knew her husband had a wandering dick and lied like it was his job. He was real good at hiding her."

Imani huffed. "So, you can see why Casey is wary of me choosing someone who might not be who they say they are."

Desmond took her hand, his eyes full of empathy. "I'm so sorry you went through that. I get your friend being concerned for you." He was silent for a moment before a playful grin spread across his face. "But...she said it was okay to sleep with me, right?"

Imani burst out laughing. "Yeah, you're cleared. She said maybe I needed a fling to get my groove back. Put me back on solid ground."

"Mmmmm. And how solid do you feel right now?"

Imani blushed as Desmond's hand trailed over her

body, leaving goosebumps in its wake. She couldn't believe how quickly he had made her forget everything she'd been worried about after walking out of Julian's funeral.

"Pretty damn solid," she replied with a smirk. She propped herself up on one elbow to look Desmond in the eye. "We're still getting to know each other, and you asked for time and I want to give you that. But please know that I care about you. I don't want this to be a sex thing. I want you to feel like this is real."

Desmond reached out and caressed Imani's skin tenderly. "You being here means a lot to me," he said. "Believing my story, standing with me, trusting me with your body, allowing me to bring you pleasure. I'm still working through some things, but I want you in my life, Imani."

He drew her into another lingering kiss, then Imani snuggled up against his broad chest, resting her head in the crook of his shoulder. She felt more content and at peace than she had in a very long time. There were still challenges and unknowns ahead, but right now, laying here in Desmond's arms, she was exactly where she wanted to be.

A while later, Imani reluctantly untangled herself from his embrace. "I should get going," she said, yawning. "But are you free this weekend? You should come over for dinner on Saturday. I will not be making ramen."

Desmond smiled. "Leave the ramen to me, sweetheart. I'd really like that. But only if you'll do me a favor."

Imani raised an eyebrow curiously. "Oh? What favor?"

"I have to do something and I could really use your support," Desmond explained. "It's nothing bad, just a little out of my comfort zone. If we have a deal, I'm all yours."

"We have a deal," Imani agreed.

She was intrigued by this mysterious errand but tried not to pry. After another long kiss goodbye, she gathered up her things and headed home, already looking forward to their weekend together.

THIRTEEN

DESMOND

HE GRIPPED the steering wheel so tightly his hands ached.

The truck came to a slow stop in front of a bungalow-style house. Though years had passed since he'd been on this street, it looked nearly identical to his childhood memories. Age showed in the faded yellow paint, crumbling concrete steps, and peeling white rails. In the time since his father moved out, the plants had become a tangled mess and the lawn was now a dry, straw-like yellow.

Desmond put the car in park and turned to Imani in the passenger seat. She gave him a gentle smile and squeezed his hand.

"Thanks for coming with me. You can still back out."

"Nope. I'm here with you. For you. It'll be fine. You ready?"

As he spoke, Desmond's throat threatened to close up. "To be honest, not really."

He stepped out of the truck and made his way up the three concrete steps to the front door. Imani walked beside him, dressed in simple dark jeans and a grey t-shirt. Her twists were pulled back into a ponytail and she wore small silver hoops in her ears. He had asked her to come along for support, but he liked the thought of arriving with a beautiful woman by his side. It gave off an aura of being put together and well-adjusted, even if he didn't feel that way.

After a momentary hesitation, he gave the door three firm knocks. The faded blue door creaked open and Roydell Taylor stood in the opening, the glow from the light behind him haloing him. He was thinner than the last time Desmond had seen him in person. He had to admit it had been longer than he would like since that had happened. Bright Pathways kept him busy and he and his father mostly connected by phone.

Still, his father had an imposing presence. It was evident that Desmond and Shawn inherited their height from him. Roydell's hair was nearly silver, trimmed short and complemented by a beard and mustache. His face lit up with a broad grin as the door opened wider.

"Desmond!" his age-worn voice rasped. "Damn, boy. Seem like you done got taller since I seen you. Who you got with you?"

"Hey, Dad. This is Imani. We're..." Desmond paused, glancing at her, then back to Roydell. "We're seeing each other."

"Well, hello, *I-ma-ni*," said Roydell, careful to enunciate every syllable of her name. He reached for her, grasping Imani's hand in both of his, and gave it a hearty shake. "Good to meet you, young lady. Come on in here."

Desmond relaxed slightly, following Roydell into the house. Stella Taylor always kept a nice home, though in recent years she hadn't had the energy for much upkeep. Now the floral sofa Desmond had napped on as a child had been replaced with a hospital bed and was flanked by two recliners. The old box TV had also been replaced by a large, mounted screen positioned at an angle so Stella could watch it from her bed.

A rolling cart sat next to her, overflowing with pill bottles, creams, bandages, and various medical equipment, including an oxygen tank connected to a cannula under her nose.

Stella lay in the bed, eyes open but glazed over and staring at an episode of *Judge Joe Brown* as if she had disappeared into her own world. Her breathing sounded wet and labored, punctuated by bouts of coughing. Her face looked pale and gaunt, her cheekbones jutting out sharply and skin hanging from the bones.

Desmond's heart was heavy. It was difficult to see his once lively, full-bodied mother reduced to a frail figure confined to a bed.

Roydell seemed to read his mind. "Stella," he called, tapping her shoulder. "Got a couple visitors here."

She slowly shifted her gaze toward the doorway. "Desmond?" Her voice was barely above a whisper, hoarse and fragile.

He approached the bed, gently lowering to sit next to her. "I heard from Shawn that you weren't feeling well, so I came by to check on you. I'm sorry it's been so long."

"That's...alright, baby," she said, a slight wheeze to each breath. "What matters...is you're here now. Glad I'm... gettin' to see you."

"Me too, Mama." He glanced behind him, waving Imani forward. "This is Imani. I met her through my job."

Imani stepped forward and laid a hand on top of Stella's. "Hello, Mrs. Taylor. It's a pleasure to meet you."

Thin fingers gripped hers and squeezed. "I ain't been... Mrs. Taylor in a while. I don't know about...how much pleasure it is...but...it's nice to meet you too." She paused to peer at Desmond. "She...a pretty one. You...thinkin' on making me...a grandmama...'fore I go?"

"Settle down, alright, Mama."

"I could deal with bein' a grandpa," said Roydell. He dropped into one of the recliners and kicked the footrest up. "Neither one of y'all being fruitful and multiplyin' to my liking."

Imani giggled, then tapped Desmond on the shoulder before stepping back.

Desmond tensed as he picked up the sound of a door opening and footsteps approaching. Shawn appeared around the corner in his shorts and a t-shirt, scratching his chest lazily. He was slender, nearly the same height as Desmond, with close cut hair and a wispy goatee on his chin.

"What up, big bro? Nice of you to drop by."

Desmond greeted him with a brief nod and a tense jaw. "Sup, Shawn. You said I had to come here, so here I am."

"Shouldn't nobody have to tell you to come see your mother," Shawn retorted, his voice rising and lip curling. "We're so lucky the saint has blessed us with his presence."

Shawn's words hit Desmond like a punch to the gut. He had expected hostility from his brother— hell, he was hostile too. But he didn't think Shawn would aim so low. Desmond rose from his spot on the bed, his jaw tense and his fists clenched at his sides. "Watch your mouth, Shawn. If I'm the saint, that makes you the opposite."

"There you go. You always gotta throw shit in my face."

Roydell waved both arms, gesturing for both men to calm down. "Let's not start this bullshit again. Every time you two get in the same room, you go at each other. Well, not today."

"Look, man, Dad's right. I'm just trying to see Mom. We can go back and forth later."

After a few painfully awkward moments, Roydell cleared his throat loudly. "Shawn, go put some clothes on, son. Your mama's medications are ready to pick up. You can go get them and be back by the time you have to go to work."

Shawn grumbled in response, his gaze still locked on Desmond. "Yeah. I'll do that. 'Cause I'm around to help, unlike your oldest."

"Enough, boy! Actin' like a child. Go on, now. Your mama needs them meds."

Desmond exhaled once Shawn disappeared again. A large part of him wanted to grab Imani and escape the discomfort and never return. Then he felt her gently squeeze his shoulder, grounding him. He resumed his seat, taking his mother's tissue-paper thin, trembling hand in both of his large, calloused ones.

"Mama, I need to apologize for staying away so long. I didn't think you wanted me around, especially after Shawn got sent away. I should have pushed through—"

"I could have been...a little more forgiving," she replied, squeezing his hand as best she could. "I was scared for Shawn. I knew you could...handle prison. I didn't know...if Shawn would make it. I was more scared...than anything. And then I was...too proud to...reach out to you. I figured you was...livin' your new life...and that was gon' be...complicated enough. I'm just...glad we got a chance...to see each other again. And..." She shot a sideways glance at Imani before returning her gaze to Desmond. "...to meet your... friend."

Desmond nodded, feeling a wave of guilt wash over him. He should have been here to support his mother, even if their relationship had been strained in the past. He should have put aside his own issues and made an effort to be there for her. But he couldn't change the past. All he could do now was try to make things right.

"Well, I'm here now if you'll have me. I know Dad and Shawn do a lot for you and I need to do my part."

"I...appreciate that. I'm gettin' tired, but...it's real...nice to see you, son."

Her eyelids slid closed. Her breathing tubes whistled with each shallow breath.

Roydell sighed from his chair. "The meds make her sleepy. Don't be a stranger, though. She needs to see you, Desmond. More than once."

"I understand," Desmond replied. "I'll be here."

The three of them moved to the kitchen, which was warm and inviting in comparison to the sterile hospital setting the living room had become. They fell into easy conversation over mugs of coffee. Desmond filled his father in on the latest at Bright Pathways and Imani's six-week project with the older teens in the group. Roydell listened attentively, his eyes shining with pride in the man his son had become.

"So...are you living here?" Desmond asked Roydell. His parents had divorced years ago, but seeing how much his mother needed help, it made sense that his father would be here.

Roydell nodded with a grim downturn of his lips. "When she got real bad, I started staying over here. It was getting too hard to manage between Shawn's schedule and a home health aide. Somebody got to be here in the off hours, so I am."

"Thanks for stepping up. You didn't tell me you were doing that."

"Don't need no award or nothin' for it. I promised her daddy I was gon' take care of her. We not married no more, but she won't leave this world by herself. That's a thing you got to know, son. A thing you need to keep in mind—seem like sooner rather than later, the way this young lady is lookin' at you."

"Dad..." Desmond felt his skin flush and his cheeks warm. "We just met—"

"Don't make no difference," Roydell said, butting in. "I know what I'm lookin' at, plain as day. Don't let pride or fear or the past get in your way. You know better than most that you got the second chance we don't all get. Make the most of it. Mmmhmmm."

He drained his mug, then tapped the table. "Y'all get on outta here. Stella will be out for a good long while. Come through in a few days, even if it's for a minute. It'll perk her up."

"Will do, Dad."

Desmond gently tucked the blankets around Stella, leaving a kiss on her forehead before he and Imani quietly exited through the front door. Shawn pulled into the driveway and climbed out of his Jeep as Desmond reached his truck.

"Short shift today?" he called.

"She's asleep. I'll be by again soon." He unlocked the passenger side door and helped Imani inside, then closed it. Before walking around to the driver's side, he paused, then backtracked to Shawn still standing on the sidewalk, holding a bag from the local pharmacy.

Meeting Shawn's eyes, he added, "I don't know how to forgive you for what happened to me. For what happened between us. I'll find a way, though. We really need to squash this so we can both be here for Mom and Dad."

Shawn seemed surprised by the unexpected statement, then nodded slowly. "Yeah. Maybe one day I'll figure out why I did it."

Back in the truck, Desmond sucked in a deep, cleansing breath, processing the afternoon. Seeing his mother, talking to his father, making headway toward forgiving Shawn. After all these years, he was finally able to offer an olive branch. It may not have been easy or fully sincere, but it was a start.

He entwined his fingers tightly with Imani's, drawing strength from her presence beside him.

"Thank you for sticking with me through that," he said. "I know it wasn't easy to witness, but trust when I say that went better than I thought it would."

Imani beamed. "You did what was necessary. I'm so proud of you." She leaned in to place a light, sweet kiss on his lips. Desmond took it further, deepening the kiss before reluctantly pulling away.

"So, what's for dinner?" he asked with a smile, revving the engine and pulling onto the road, feeling a weight lifted off his shoulders that he hadn't felt in years.

They drove back to his place to retrieve her car, and then he trailed behind her as they made their way across town to her mid-rise condo building. The stark contrasts between his neighborhood and hers made him uneasy.

He followed Imani into the lobby, where they took the elevator up to her floor. They walked down a plush carpeted hallway until they reached her condo, a corner unit. Desmond took in her home with wide-eyed curiosity.

The spacious living room was tastefully decorated with expensive furnishings and pieces of art and full bookcases. The kitchen gleamed with stainless steel appliances and marble countertops.

Even pre-prison, he'd never lived this well.

"Make yourself at home," Imani said. She kicked off her sneakers and carried them off into another room. "I already know you think it's bougie. It's nice, but it's just stuff."

"Not judging, just admiring. I think my studio could fit in your living room. You've done well for yourself."

Desmond wandered around for a bit before making himself comfortable on the couch, taking in the stunning view of the skyline from the floor to-ceiling windows. Imani reappeared with two glasses and a liquor bottle, then sat next to him.

"I'm not much of a brown drinker, but I had a feeling today was going to take some wind out of you. Casey told me what to get."

He picked up the bottle, inspecting the label and giving an approving nod. "She got good taste," he said, cracking the seal on the bottle of Macallan scotch, pouring them each a healthy sip.

"Thank you," he said, lifting his glass. "For this," he added. "For today."

"I was just along for the ride," she countered, sipping from her glass. "But you're welcome."

Desmond offered a lopsided smile and took a long swig of the warming amber liquid. "There was a time when I would sit on my bed with my back against a stone wall, mindlessly watching some TV show on a tiny screen. I used to dream about sitting on a leather couch, gazing out at the city skyline and enjoying a few sips of this smooth brown liquor with a beautiful woman."

"And now you're here, doing just that. What will you daydream of next?" Imani asked, scooting closer to him, her knee nudging his thigh.

He set his glass down on the coffee table and turned to face her, eyes smoldering. "I think I'll show you how much I appreciate all you've done for me this week. Starting with this," he said, leaning in to capture her lips.

Imani didn't protest as the kiss deepened, wrapping her arms around his neck and pulling him closer. Just as she was about to suggest they move to a more comfortable location, her stomach made its loud complaint of a long, emotional day with no food.

In unison, they both burst into laughter.

"We can pick that up later," said Imani, swinging her legs off of the couch and bouncing toward the kitchen.

"Sounds like a plan," he replied, his tone husky and body craving her but willing to put it off in the immediate for a payoff later.

Desmond hovered awkwardly, unsure what to do with himself. Imani pulled out a dish of marinating chicken from the refrigerator, followed by a few bags of fresh vegetables. He recognized the bags from the DeKalb Farmers Market.

Imani smirked, waving him into the kitchen. "Two days ago, you had your face between my legs, and today I met your mother. Don't get shy on me now. Wash your hands. Jump in. Do you need an apron?"

Desmond shuffled into the kitchen where Imani had staged the long, wide peninsula to chop vegetables. She bumped her hip playfully against his.

"Music? A movie? What would help you relax right now?"

"Uh, music would be great."

She pulled an apron from a drawer and handed it to

him, then headed to a small panel on the wall. A press of a button filled the kitchen with old-school R&B hits. He bobbed his head while slipping the apron over his head and tying it around his waist. "The '99 and the 2000."

Imani laughed as she handed him a knife and a cutting board. "Start chopping."

The two of them worked comfortably, occasionally bumping into each other while swaying to the music. Desmond admired Imani's ease and grace in the kitchen as she effortlessly moved between tasks and ingredients.

"So...you said you were getting back into cooking. How'd you fall off?"

Imani sighed, her back still turned to him as she adjusted the temperature on the gas range. "I got lazy. I started working long hours. Then I was dating Julian, who was here every other weekend, and he *loved* Atlanta restaurants. Even when he wasn't here, if I ever mentioned that I was hungry or tired, he would have something delivered to me. Eating out instead of cooking became a bad habit that was hard to break."

"Well, I don't have a lot of cash for dinners out and delivery orders," said Desmond, "but I have enjoyed doing my own cooking the past few years. I'd be happy to help you keep breaking that habit. I promise I cook more than prison ramen."

Imani turned, wiping her hands on a towel, and walked over to where he was chopping peppers. She stepped behind him and drew her arms around his waist, then laid her head on his back.

"Deal. I've missed cooking for someone I care about."

FOURTEEN

DESMOND

DESMOND LEANED back in his chair and tapped his belly, pleasantly full from the Thai chicken and noodles Imani had prepared. Lemongrass, chili, and fresh basil flavors lingered on his tongue as he watched her begin clearing the table. Dinner had been intimate and romantic, the conversation jumping from topic to topic, a testament to their growing comfort with each other.

"That was delicious," he said, his eyes locked on her hips swaying to Aretha Franklin as she took the plates to the kitchen.

"I'm glad you liked it. It's a recipe I found online and wanted to try. Definitely going in the rotation."

"I should help you with this," he offered, standing to gather the plates and serving dishes.

Imani waved him off. "Next time. Tonight, you're my guest," she said, pouring him a fresh glass of iced tea and nudging him out of the dining room. "This will just take a minute. Go in the living room. Relax."

He complied, settling on the couch while Imani made pleasant humming noises along with the music. His gaze drifted to the windows and the glittering midtown skyline. He was for sure out of his element, but Imani didn't make him feel as if he didn't belong.

She reappeared after a while, curling up beside him on the couch. "So...not to poke the bear, but how are you feeling about today? It had to be emotional seeing your mom again after so long."

Desmond took a sip, contemplating. "I'll be honest, that was rough," he admitted. "Part of the reason is because she's literally not the same person. She's nowhere near the stoic woman that would come with my dad to see me at Jesup. She's not the angry battle ax that almost cursed me out when Shawn was sentenced. She's just...not the woman I remember."

He shook his head. "Even though she pretty much told me to go to hell for sending her baby son to prison, I shouldn't have stayed away for so long. I knew she was sick and it was going to get worse. I don't know what I expected—"

"Don't be so hard on yourself," Imani said gently. "If the situation were different, do you think you'd be making amends?"

"Maybe. Can't say. Time does so much to heal wounds and suck the emotion out of a situation. It was good to talk to my dad, though." A faint smile crossed his lips. "We haven't had a face-to-face conversation in a long time. You close to your folks?"

Imani nodded. "Yeah. We don't talk as often as we used to, but yeah. I heard what you said to Shawn. Is there any hope of reconciling with him? Do you even want to?"

At the mention of Shawn, a vein in his forehead pulsed and his jaw clenched. Old wounds ran deep. "We have a long way to go. I'll say that. I know I need to forgive him, especially with Mom being sick. But that won't come easy, and he..."

He exhaled heavily. "His attitude doesn't help."

Imani squeezed his arm reassuringly. "No one expects it to be easy. I'm proud of you for reaching across the aisle at all." He covered her hand with his. A few moments of thoughtful silence passed before Imani spoke again. "You seem deep inside your head lately. Talk to me."

Desmond considered brushing her off again, but there was no point in pretending, and eventually, she would find out.

"There is a chance that Bright Pathways could be in danger of closing," he confessed. "Not next week or next month, and it's not even guaranteed, but just the threat makes me worry. The *AJC* is reporting that the governor is proposing budget cuts next year. We might have to scale way back or cut staff. Or...even shut down completely."

Saying the words out loud sent a fresh wave of anxiety through him.

Imani's eyes flooded with concern. "Desmond...I'm so sorry. I didn't know."

"I know. I'm not trying to dump on you. It's just eating me up inside. Kids of all ages depend on the center. It's the one place that gives them a positive, safe space to be. It gives them hope, it keeps them off the streets. If funding gets pulled and I can't replace it..."

He dragged a hand down his face. "I'll feel like I failed them."

"You could never fail them," Imani insisted, shifting closer to him on the couch. "Look how they sought you out when Caesar was arrested. You've gained their trust and that's hard to do with teenagers. Don't discount that."

Desmond smiled faintly at her encouragement. "I don't. I just wish I didn't feel like I'd be letting them down. And letting me down. The center is all I've got. My purpose, my redemption after...everything. If it's gone, then what?"

Imani took both his hands in hers, her dark eyes brimming with empathy. "I know Bright Pathways means a lot to you, and it should. It is your life's work and you should be proud of it, but Desmond, baby...your worth isn't defined by that center. You're so much more than your past or your present or what anyone thinks you owe. Don't lose sight of that."

Her words pierced his heart. He drew a shaky breath, overcome with emotions he couldn't put into words.

"There's the silver lining," Imani said. "It's not over yet. Not even close. We'll find a way through this. In fact..."

She paused, drawing her bottom lip between her teeth. The wheels in her mind were clearly turning. "I ...my brain is already popping with ideas. I can put my resources behind analyzing the books and I can work to raise funds. Let me research grant and investment opportunities—I'd love to be part of the effort to keep the center open."

Desmond stared at her in wonderment. "For real? Like...past the six-week required pro bono project?"

"Yes," she said, rolling her eyes. "Consider me part of the team. Casey too. She's excellent at research and she's a great wingwoman. Besides, she's dying to meet you."

Profound gratitude welled in Desmond's chest and threatened to bust it wide open. Her help could mean he'd have a fighting chance at saving Bright Pathways.

"I don't even know what to say besides thank you."

"Of course," she replied. "We're in this together now."

Together. The word resonated. He didn't take it lightly.

Desmond had struggled alone for a long time. Now, with Imani so earnestly offering not only help but companionship, he didn't have to shoulder his burdens solo anymore. His chest ached with the realization of just how much he cared for her, of how right it felt to be with her. He wanted her—needed her in every sense of the word.

"So, uhmmm..." Imani stroked a nonexistent crumb from his cheek. "What are you about to do?"

Heat flooded Desmond's veins at the question. Without a word, he drew her up from the couch and into his arms. Imani melted against him, fingers trailing down his chest in a featherlight caress. Unable to resist any longer, he dipped to capture her lips in a kiss. Her eager response sent shockwaves through him, eliciting just the reaction he was hoping for.

When the kiss broke, Desmond rested his forehead against hers, struggling to rein in his runaway emotions. He was barreling into uncharted territory and despite the warning bells in his head, he was powerless to fight the connection growing between them.

Imani seemed to read his mind. She cradled his face in her hands, eyes shining up at him. "You're not trying to go home, are you?" she whispered.

Every ounce of reason told Desmond this was dangerous—for his heart, his focus, his sense of discipline. But with her curves pressed against him and her intoxicating scent clouding his senses, resistance was futile.

He shook his head. "I'm about to do *you*, if that's alright."

Imani's eyes widened. "That's more than alright."

Taking her hand, he allowed himself to be led down the hallway. They crossed the threshold into her bedroom, the rest of the world falling away. Tangled in her embrace with moonlight streaming through the windows, there was only this moment, this woman, this feeling of wholeness he'd never known.

Imani's lips were plump and inviting as they explored his neck, her touch setting his skin ablaze. He groaned at the sensation, arching into her as she trailed kisses down his chest. Desmond's every nerve ending was on fire, her touch like a brand searing him permanently.

His breath stuttered as she moved lower still, teasing him through the thin fabric of his boxer briefs. He gripped the sheets as he struggled to maintain control, knowing that once he surrendered to her, there would be no going back.

But then she was peeling away his boxers and taking him into her mouth with a skill that left him gasping for air. His fingers tangled in her hair as she worked him expertly, building a steady rhythm that threatened to undo him entirely.

"Got *damn*, you're good at that."

Imani moaned seductively, her lips and tongue slick and sinfully talented, taking him to the edge of oblivion with each stroke.

Desmond couldn't resist her any longer. He flipped them over so that she was beneath him, her legs spread invitingly. He lined himself up with her, catching the smoky gaze in her eyes.

Then he was inside, inch by agonizing inch until they were fully connected. Imani writhed beneath him, clutching and clinging to him as he began to move. The rhythm was urgent and raw, each thrust driving them both higher. A mind-blowing release was building and threatening to break at any moment.

He held on, determined to make this last. He wanted every second with Imani burned into his memory forever. Her name was a whisper on his lips as they moved in perfect unison, bodies slick with sweat and desire. When she finally shattered, pulsing around him, Desmond followed suit, spilling inside her with a roar.

They stayed tangled together, the weight of her body against his before finally separating and collapsing next to one another. Neither spoke for several long moments as they came down from the euphoric high.

Desmond had broken every rule he'd established for himself after his release from prison. He had recklessly allowed himself to become emotionally attached to someone despite the fragility of relationships. He had taken a dangerous gamble that could potentially undo all his hard work.

But Imani had done what he'd thought was impossible—she had made him feel hope again. She had made him look forward to the future again.

She had made him feel, for the first time in his life, like he was falling in love. That terrified him as much as it exhilarated him.

For tonight, though, he pushed fear, hesitation, and any thoughts that he didn't deserve this moment aside and pulled her spent, sweaty form close.

FIFTEEN

IMANI

"HI, DENISE!"

The click of Imani's strappy heels echoed down the hallway as she greeted the afternoon receptionist and approached the lounge of Bright Pathways, a bag from Piece of Cake in one hand and her leather bag hanging off of an arm. She had chosen her outfit carefully—a silky dress that accentuated her curves and shimmery gold pumps.

Pushing open the double doors, she was greeted by the familiar chaos of the after-school program. Bodies were sprawled across the couches. Teens were chatting or playing games, while others laughed as they sat around one of several tables. Across the room, Desmond sat at his desk, deep in discussion with a student. As soon as she entered, his head swiveled around. When their eyes met, his handsome face lit up with a smile.

"You need to gimme that dress, Ms. Imani. It's fire!"

All eyes turned to admire Imani's dress as she gave a

little twirl, the flared skirt fanning out to reveal a hint of leg. She laughed, warmed by Deja's always effusive commentary on her attire. "Thank you, Deja. I can always count on you to appreciate the look. Fire is good, right?"

She handed the bag to Desmond, wishing she could drop a kiss on his lips and get a long, tight hug like the one he'd given her when he left her place the night before. They'd been practically inseparable since the weekend. So much had changed between them, and all it took was a six-week work project that she had initially dreaded, then come to love.

"Ms. Imani brought you hooligans some cupcakes," said Desmond, spreading the boxes out among the group. The students eagerly dug in, grabbing decadent vanilla cupcakes piled high with frosting and an edible 'BP' charm.

"I can't believe this is our final session," she began, clasping her hands as she stood at the front of the room. "And it took me this long to figure out how to keep you all quiet."

The room erupted in good-natured laughter.

"Before we dive into today's session, I want to thank you all for these past six weeks together. You've enriched my life immensely."

"We gon' miss you, Ms. Imani," said Caleb around a mouthful of cupcake. The other teens voiced their agreement.

"I'd normally say I'll miss you all, too," Imani replied, pausing for dramatic effect, then glancing at Desmond, whose sneaky, devilish smile spread across his face. "But fortunately, while this is the last session of this series, this isn't goodbye forever. Desmond and I have had a few great conversations about the changes that we could effect here together and...I'll be sticking around."

Gasps and exclamations of joy filled the lounge, along with a few shouts of "Yes!"

"I thought you'd all like that." Her eyes swept across the group, meeting each teen's gaze. "So, our last discussion of this series will be an opening salvo to our continuing relationship. Just like you see Desmond as a valuable resource and partner, I want you to think of me in the same way. I am here for you whenever you need guidance or support. So..."

Imani dragged a chair close to him and took a seat. "Let's have an open Q&A session. Ask me anything about life after high school— jobs, money, education, relationships. I'm here to help in any way I can."

Desmond gave an approving nod as eager hands shot up around the room.

"Deja?" Imani called out.

"Okay, for real," Deja began, "it's kinda scary thinking about turning eighteen. Graduating high school. Thinking about what to do after that. Like...what if I get kicked out of my foster home?"

"Is that a valid concern with a high likelihood, or are you covering your bases?"

"Covering my bases, mostly. But I want to be prepared if something goes down."

"Nothing wrong with being ready. If you stay ready, you don't have to..."

"Get ready!" the kids finished.

"Good job. We've been talking for the last six weeks about getting your budget together, opening a savings account, figuring out your wants versus your needs to establish a budget. If you want to do another segment on looking for a place to live, exploring options for employment, or government assistance, we can map that out."

Desmond nodded in agreement, adding, "Seriously—

housing, food, job help. Between Imani and I, we know people and we can research resources that can help you out. Let us connect you to the community."

Deja's expression flattened as though a weight had been lifted off her shoulders. "I was thinking about going to community college, then transferring somewhere. Can you get scholarships and loans for that?"

"You sure can. While we're talking, I'd love to connect you with someone in purchasing at a department store, get you in on the ground floor of fashion and merchandising."

Deja gasped, clapping her hands together. "That would be dope!"

Time seemed to pass quickly as the group discussed their futures—Caleb's dream of opening a barber shop, Deja's burgeoning fashion career, and Caesar's plan to put his sales experience to work legitimately and open his own business. Desmond chimed in now and again with advice and resources.

Imani glanced at her watch, dismayed to see just how late it had gotten. Desmond stepped in to redirect the discussion.

"Okay, everyone, that's it for tonight. We've kept you way over time. So—"

"Wait. One last question."

All heads turned to see Chloe, a quiet student who always sat in the back of the room.

"First, thanks for coming to talk with us," she said. "I like seeing somebody that looks like me as a success story. Sometimes I feel like ain't no way these folks gonna let me work in medicine, even though I show aptitude for science and physiology. You helped me feel like thinking that way is dumb. I can do anything I want to do."

Tears pricked Imani's eyes. "You're very welcome, and

yes, you can do whatever you put your mind to. What's your question, honey?"

"Uhm... Are you and Desmond gonna like...date? 'Cause the vibes are *immaculate*."

Laughter erupted around the room. Imani felt a blush creeping into her cheeks and Desmond, who had taken a bite of cupcake, nearly choked as he sputtered.

"First of all," said Imani, "that's none of your business."

"You said ask you anything," Caleb protested. "That's anything."

"And you said if you couldn't answer, you'd come back with the answer," said Deja. "So?"

Imani chuckled nervously. "I—" She glanced at Desmond for support, but he was too busy laughing. "Are... what should we—"

"Man, I thought y'all were smart," Desmond teased, sucking his teeth. "Y'all slow."

"Whatchu mean, slow?" asked Caleb, sitting up.

"Wait! What..." Deja began, eyes widening.

Caleb hopped up, punching his fist in the air. "Aye! I knew it!"

"You ain't know shit!" said Caesar.

"So y'all are already..." Chloe began, then trailed off. She rebounded with, "Get it, Mr. Desmond."

Imani's cheeks were inflamed. "We are seeing where this goes and liking where we're headed so far."

"Y'all waited way too long to get to the juicy shit. Should have started with that question. Anything else you want to confess before we go?" Caesar asked as they all laughed.

Desmond stretched out his hand and grasped Imani's, sending a shiver down her spine. "Nah, man. I think we'll keep the rest to ourselves. You guys get out of here. Have a great Friday."

After the last teens departed, strong arms encircled Imani's waist from behind. She melted into Desmond's embrace with a contented sigh, inhaling his scent.

"You have been amazing with these kids," he murmured, nuzzling her neck.

"It's definitely all them. I just made it a point to listen. You know that trick too."

"Don't sell yourself short. You've done a lot in a few short weeks. Not just for them, for me too."

Heart swelling, she turned in his arms, then rose on tiptoe to brush her lips tenderly against his. Sparks danced through her veins at the contact.

Just then, exaggerated throat-clearing sounded from the doorway. Breaking apart, they turned to see several faces peeking in, poorly concealing giggles and snickers.

"Busted!" Desmond chuckled, pulling Imani closer.

"It's some sneakin' and freakin' up in here!" Deja crowed. "Y'all cute as hell, though."

Desmond and Imani exchanged warm looks. "You hear that? We're cute as hell."

Wolf whistles and cheers ensued before Imani shooed them away in mock indignation. "Don't y'all have some-where to be? Away from here?"

Still snickering, the teens departed for the second time. Desmond drew Imani closer, tight up against him. "Appar-ently we should have waited until they were good and out the door."

She giggled as he captured her mouth in a lingering kiss that left her breathless. When they finally parted, his eyes smoldered.

"So...what you about to do?" he asked, voice husky.

Imani pretended to ponder. "Mmmm...I thought I'd spend time with this great guy I've been seeing."

Desmond quirked a brow. "You mean me, right?"

"Can I...ask you a favor?" Imani whispered, trailing a finger down his chest.

"You could ask me for anything right about now, Imani."

"Good, because I haven't been able to stop thinking about your damn prison ramen. I need you to make me a bowl without picking on me about it."

Throwing his head back, Desmond laughed. "I told you it was good, didn't I?"

"You may gloat all night, so long as you're making me a bowl of ramen while you do so."

At Desmond's place, Imani wasted no time getting comfortable. She kicked off her shoes, then rifled through Desmond's drawers until she found a pair of sweats and a t-shirt to change into. After that, she pulled a travel toiletry kit from her bag and disappeared into the bathroom.

A few minutes later, she reappeared fresh-faced with a coat of Vaseline on her lips and her hair pulled back. She flopped onto the couch and grabbed the remote, pointing it at the TV to pull up a lo-fi music channel on YouTube.

Desmond was busy in the kitchen, the steam from a pot of water dissipating into the air. He chopped vegetables and sautéed cuts of pork before breaking open two packets of noodles and dropping them into the water. Soon, the rich aroma of spices enveloped the studio. Desmond presented her with a piping hot bowl piled high with noodles, juicy pork, and vegetables.

"My famous ramen, by request," he said, setting the bowl in front of her on the coffee table. "Do you mind if I take over the TV? I wanted to catch a few minutes of a live broadcast I usually watch."

"Go for it. I'm starving and my face is going to be in this bowl."

Desmond picked up the laptop, then found the broadcast he was looking for and cast it to the TV. They ate, sipping the savory broth and winding the noodles up with chopsticks while watching the Thursday evening live show on Beyond Bars.

The host, a chiseled man with tattoos peeking out from under a crisp blue button-up and silver-rimmed glasses, led a panel of previously incarcerated men through discussions about current events, pop culture, and their own personal growth post-release.

Among the guests were two brothers who had spent time in different prisons, then were coincidentally released within months of each other. After their release, one had pursued a passion for spirits and opened a successful craft beer brewery with his wife. The other was studying to become a chef, utilizing some techniques he had learned while working in the prison kitchen. These men were more than ex-convicts; they were articulate, intelligent, and fully engaged in a world that had changed so much since their last taste of freedom.

"These guys have a great story," Imani commented. She drank the last of the broth from her bowl and set it down on the table.

"Yeah, I've been following their story for a while. They come on a lot, share their progress, especially with the ones fresh out. It's a culture shock if you've been away for longer than a few years. Coming back out requires a lot of support."

They finished watching the show and Desmond turned off the TV. Imani leaned back on the couch.

"Have you ever gone on this show? Told your story?"

she asked, breaking the comfortable silence that had settled between them.

Desmond shook his head, a shy half-smile on his lips as he set his bowl down on the table. "Nah. I didn't talk about my bid a lot because I didn't want it to blow back on the kids or the center. Even though I was exonerated, all people will see is the prison sentence. I also don't want to use these kids and the center as a crutch or something I get praise for. I do this work because I really want to do it. I don't want to use it for notoriety."

Imani nodded in understanding but also felt frustrated by his words. Despite being exonerated for years, Desmond's time in prison and wrongful conviction continued to weigh heavily on him. She was aware that part of his hesitation to open up about his experience stemmed from not wanting to be perceived as a victim or as courting pity.

She reached out and took his hand in hers, their fingers intertwining.

"I hear you," she said softly. "I do. But I think the way you live your life keeps you in a certain mindset—almost like you still have a sentence to serve. You paid your debt for a crime you didn't even commit, Desmond. You deserve to be proud of that. You deserve to live life as a free man. You deserve to be happy."

Desmond looked at her for a long moment before leaning over and dropping a gentle kiss on her forehead.

"I am happy," he whispered. "Right here, right now. Or in the afternoon at the center, or on the weekends at your place, or over at my mom's place...I'm happy."

With a gentle squeeze of his hand, she whispered, "All I want is for you to have that. It's what you deserve."

Later, limbs tangled together beneath the sheets on the

slim bed, Imani marveled at how she could have ever thought of Desmond as someone to keep at a distance. Her heart had undergone a metamorphosis these past weeks. What began as a fling had blossomed into something profoundly meaningful with amazing potential.

For the first time in weeks, Julian's image flashed across her mind. She chuckled, blinking him away. He was firmly her past now. Her future was laying next to her with an arm flung over his forehead, worn out and lightly snoring.

She nuzzled into the crook of his shoulder and pulled the blanket up higher, cocooned in contentment. The future brimmed with possibility, but of one thing she was certain—she had taken the biggest risk of her life and come out on top.

Now she was exactly where she wanted and needed to be.

EPILOGUE- ONE YEAR LATER

IMANI

IMANI BEAMED as she watched the halls of Bright Pathways fill with people, young and old. Their chatter and laughter brightened the building, already buzzing with activity. Summer Day Camp had launched, and the lounge was packed with kids playing games, working on art projects, or hanging out. Sunlight streamed through the windows, the room practically glowing with cheerful energy.

When the governor's proposed budget cuts hit earlier that year, operating funds for the center were cut in half, threatening to close the center's doors for good. Imani, Desmond, and Casey had rallied with a plan already in place.

There were so many nights spent at Imani's dining room table with grant applications stacked on one half, remnants of dinner they'd cooked together on the other. There were weekends planning and attending fundraising events with emotionally charged speeches from the people who knew it best—the attendees. Caesar had become a local celebrity after sharing his story of how spending one weekend in jail had been enough to keep him on the path to success. Even Conrad, her boss, had made a hefty donation from Richardson & Burke.

Bright Pathways would get by on a bare-bones budget and lots of community goodwill for at least another year… until Imani checked her mail and nearly passed out when she opened an envelope from a Raleigh, North Carolina law firm. Despite his widow's protests, Julian had left Imani a small sum in his will. It wasn't much compared to the Carver family fortune, but to Imani, the unexpected windfall meant another few months of operation for Bright Pathways and the ability to fund an incredible summer program.

"Hey, beautiful," murmured a deep voice in her ear as strong arms closed around her waist. Imani's shoulders instantly dropped as she sank back into Desmond's embrace with a contented sigh.

"Hey, yourself." She smiled, tilting her head to the side, giving him access to her neck. "You're here early."

"Missed you. Couldn't wait to see you," he said, lips brushing against her earlobe.

The past year had been a proving ground for them and they were still going strong. The electricity between them was impossible for anyone around them to deny.

Desmond made her happier than she'd ever dreamed possible. Their shared devotion to running the center together only strengthened the bond between them. She split her time between his cozy studio and her condo, and they had just closed on a home not far from Bright Pathways. Desmond and his father were completing repairs and painting before they moved in the following weekend.

Since Stella's passing six months prior, Roydell had time to fill, so he was often in and out of the center with his toolbox and tool belt. He was also renovating Stella's house and yard so it could be sold. Shawn had taken a job that kept him busy. He'd moved out and now rented a house with friends.

Desmond planted a long, sloppy kiss on her cheek. "These kids are having a blast. You did a great job putting the day camp together."

"*We* did, babe," she corrected, turning to face him. "It was a team effort."

"Alright, I'll take some credit. I sharpened your pencils for you." Their lips met in a tender kiss and for a moment, the noise in the room seemed to recede. "Can you take a break? I'm craving you," Desmond murmured close to her ear, his hands gently caressing her back.

Imani glanced around the bustling room. "I'm technically on the clock—"

"Ugh, get a room!" Deja called out teasingly as she rushed by. She'd graduated high school and started her first year at Perimeter College and worked part-time at Bright Pathways. "I got this. Y'all go somewhere."

Desmond gave her hand a squeeze. "Let's take five."

Imani's heart smiled, looking around. The center hadn't just been saved—it was thriving. She thought of the sleepless nights planning fundraising events, the tearful interviews with the local news, the impassioned speeches to donors. And the letters...all of the letters she'd written, printed, and mailed out.

The effort had been worth it.

Her work was more than spreadsheets and PowerPoint presentations and yawn-inducing meetings with corporate bigwigs—though she did still have to endure those tasks.

Now she could clock out and spend her time in a place where she knew she was making a difference.

She glanced at the man she'd fallen in love with. She also had love and support. Who could ask for more?

"We'll be back in a little bit."

"Take your time," Deja said as she bent over a table to help two children get started at the art table. "We'll be fine."

Imani and Desmond headed to the office that Roydell had framed and enclosed in a far corner of the center. He closed the door behind them and locked it.

Desmond's grin was full of mischief as he backed Imani against the wall, his hands roaming over her hips and up her shirt, fingers slipping underneath her bra to caress her silky skin.

"I was over at the house this morning," he said, his voice a husky whisper in her ear. He traced a finger along her collarbone before gently nibbling on her neck, eliciting a moan from deep within her. "I've been thinking all day about how excited I am to be living with you in *our* place."

"Mmmm," she purred, wrapping her arms around his neck. "That does sound nice. No more shuffling stuff from one end of town to the other."

"Not that I mind. I'd shuffle my stuff anywhere to be with you. And just think..." His lips traveled down to her chest as he unbuttoned her shirt. "You get prison ramen whenever you want it."

"That..." Imani let out a gasp as his lips found their way to one of her sensitive spots. "That sounds like heaven to me."

"Imani," he murmured against her skin. "I love you so much."

Her heart swelled at those three words. She knew they

were true every time he said them but hearing them still gave her butterflies.

"I love you too, Desmond," she whispered back before pulling him in for another kiss. "I love you so much."

I AM SO grateful to readers who take the time to pick up my books. Thank you for reading Calculated Risk! If you enjoyed it, help spread the word by offering a review at your favorite social media site, a retail sales site (where applicable) and Goodreads, Fable or The Storygraph.

Want to be the first to know about upcoming novels, cover reveals, contests, giveaway and new releases? Join my newsletter at Booksbydlwhite.com/newsletter.

Find all the links you'll ever need for Books by DL White on my Links page- booksbydlwhite.com/linkinbio.

In the mood for a quick shot of romance? Pick up my Valentine's Day themed novella Grumpy Valentine, available in ebook, print or audio!

ACKNOWLEDGMENTS

Here we are at the end of another *Books by DL White* project. As I always say, I'm sure there are legion of people that belong in these acknowledgments, but I also always say that my brain is Swiss cheese and paperclips.

My endless gratitude goes to the formerly incarcerated individuals who share their experiences of rebuilding their lives, finding purpose, and discovering love despite society's judgment. Your courage to start your lives over inspired every page of this book.

To the dedicated staff and volunteers at community centers and at-risk programs across the country creating safe spaces for our youth: thank you for showing me what it means to give back. I know from past personal experience working with AmeriCorps in underserved communities that the work you do changes lives.

Thank you to AdotK Edits, who helped me shape and polish Desmond and Imani's love story with heart and a little humor. I never dread the edit!

Huge thanks to Ian Bick, whose podcast Locked In with Ian Bick was the catalyst for Desmond's story and his redemption. Ian's own story and his show gave me inspiration for the fictional *Beyond Bars* group and its members.

Special thanks to my family for their always unwavering support, and to my friends/chosen family who keep me grounded while encouraging me to reach higher. You know who you are.

And last, because they're closest to my heart, thank you to my readers: I hope this story reminds you that authentic love grows from understanding, acceptance, and the courage to be vulnerable. May we all get endless chances at love and happiness.

XoXo,
DL White

BOOKS BY DL WHITE

Find Books and Merch at Booksbydlwhite.com/shop

Brunch at Ruby's, a Ruby's novel

Dinner at Sam's, a Ruby's novel

Beach Thing, a Black Diamond Romance

Elysium, a Black Diamond Vacation Romance

The Pearl at Black Diamond, a Black Diamond Romance

Leslie's Curl & Dye, a Potter Lake Small Town Romance

Second Time Around, a Potter Lake Holiday Short

The Guy Next Door, a Potter Lake Small Town Romance

Home for the Holidays, A Potter Lake Holiday Novella

The Kwanzaa Brunch, a Holiday Short

A Thin Line

The Never List

Hey, Lover, a Second Chance Romance

Unexpected, a holiday short

The Festival at Evergreen Falls

Grumpy Valentine, a Holiday Novella

www.ingramcontent.com/pod-product-compliance
Lightning Source LLC
Chambersburg PA
CBHW020641250626
47154CB00008B/2767